A CANDLELIGHT ECSTASY ROMANCE

"I've never let anyone get this close."

Her voice faltered. Nick took her trembling hand in his, letting his strong fingers intertwine with her own. "I need to know you," he murmured.

Abby stared at him, searching his face for some sign, something that would reassure her. His brown eyes never left her luminous gray ones until his dark head lowered and his mouth claimed hers with a stamp of possession. Abby's lips parted willingly, letting her tongue explore and taste the sweetness of her own hungry desire. She moaned softly, responding willingly and naturally to his intimate caresses as the rising heat of dormant desire shuddered through her body. . . .

Dear Reader:

In response to your enthusiasm for Candlelight Ecstasy Romances, we are now increasing the number of titles per month from two to three.

We are pleased to offer you sensuous novels set in America depicting modern American women and men as they confront the provocative problems of a modern relationship.

Throughout the history of the Candlelight line, Dell has tried to maintain a high standard of excellence, to give you the finest in reading pleasure. It is now and will remain our most ardent ambition.

Vivian Stephens
Editor
Candlelight Romances

TENDER YEARNINGS

Elaine Raco Chase

A CANDLELIGHT ECSTASY ROMANCE

Special thanks to

Evie Williams
WINDHAM, N.H.

and

Madeline Longacker
CLIFTON PARK, N.Y.

Published by
Dell Publishing Co., Inc.
1 Dag Hammarskjold Plaza
New York, New York 10017

ISBN: 0-440-18552-1

Printed in the United States of America

First printing—August 1981

CHAPTER ONE

Dominick Maxwell Bennett surveyed the lineup of cold remedies that stood like miniature militia men atop his wide oak desk. There was the package of time capsules that guaranteed relief for twelve hours but faded after five; the eight-hour nasal spray that allowed you to breathe freely for only half that time; the superstrength cough medicine laced with decongestant that made him feel dizzy even when he was sitting down. Wearily, Dominick rubbed a large hand over his rugged features, feeling more than double his thirty-six years, and reached for another bitter-tasting horehound throat lozenge.

"Hold it," interrupted a lilting feminine voice, "the advertising department has sent you its version of the perfect cold remedy."

Dominick looked up to find his executive assistant, Ann Learner, standing in the doorway. "I'm not sure

I can live through any more home remedies," he grumbled thickly. "What is it this time?" He watched her neat, beige suit-clad figure stride farther into the sumptuous brown and gold executive office.

"After you spent the morning coughing and sneezing, the copywriters took up a collection and sent you this," Ann told him with undisguised amusement, adding two more containers to the lineup cluttering his desk top. "A quart of orange juice and one hundred Vitamin C tablets with rose hips."

Dominick's good-natured chuckle quickly turned into a deep, hacking cough.

Ann frowned, shaking her silver-streaked head in disgust. "You know," she admonished with motherly concern, passing Dominick a spoon for the cough medicine, "as president, you are entitled to the same number of sick days that the rest of your employees receive."

"I'm just the acting president," he reminded her hoarsely, making a face after swallowing the thick mixture.

"You still qualify for all company benefits," she retorted with exasperation. "By the way, about your aftershave—" Two fingers came up to pinch her nose.

"It's Mrs. Hickock's camphor cure," Dominick grinned. "That's what happens when you have an English housekeeper."

"The smell will either cure you or kill you." Ann laughed.

"Anything really earth-shattering in the afternoon

8

mail?" he inquired, returning the assorted cold preparations to his bottom desk drawer.

Ann shook her head. "July is a rather quiet month. Everyone's on vacation, with business the furthest thing from their minds. We did get a postcard from your father."

"And where is the recuperating company president this month?" he inquired, relaxing in the comfort of his brown contoured chair.

"It seems he's jumped ship, if you can call a luxury liner that," Ann told him, handing him a gaily colored picture postcard. "He's prowling the Hawaiian Islands before he heads home to New York."

"Well, I just hope he gets in some rest and relaxation." Dominick frowned thoughtfully. "That's why he decided to take the cruise. Even a mild heart attack is one hell of a shock to a body's system."

Ann snorted derisively. "Your father is a fraud."

"What makes you say that?" His dark brows jumped at her bald statement.

"Dom, I've worked with John Bennett for over thirty-five years. I know him better than I know my own husband." She smiled softly, her hazel eyes mirroring her memories fondly. "I watched him turn a small tri-state credit company into a huge corporation taking in the entire Eastern seaboard. Despite all his business interests, his family always came first. He was devastated when your mother died, which only made him draw closer to his only child. When you took that job as a foreign correspondent for the wire service and went overseas, I could see the change in him."

9

Ann waved Dominick's interruption aside. "He threw all his energy into the company. John was speeding right to the top; and suddenly, lots of very cunning ladies noticed the very attractive widower who was president of Charge-X. Your father's so-called heart attack was a chronic case of indigestion coupled with late hours after turning into a sixty-five-year-old playboy!"

"You are serious." He gaped at her in open astonishment.

"Very," Ann returned bluntly. "You fell right into his trap by offering to give up your overseas assignment and take over Charge-X while he recuperated."

Dominick gave a rueful laugh. "I often wondered why the doctor's reports I asked him for always seemed to get sidetracked. How long was this charade supposed to go on?"

Ann's answer was interrupted by the agitated figure of Bill York, who rushed past the receptionist into the office.

"Mr. Bennett, something has to be done!" Bill exploded angrily. "This is the fourth time the entire state of Virginia has been wiped out of the computers!"

Dominick stared at the short, stocky young man through feverish, watery eyes. "Who, what, when, where, and how?" he questioned listlessly, motioning him into a nearby chair.

"I've finally traced the problem to account forty-three stroke eighty-one stroke seventy—"

"Names, Bill, give me a real name!" Dominick's voice croaked gruffly. Bill York, the extremely competent head of the computer billing division, had always struck his boss as rather excitable and melodramatic whenever he had to deal with people and not his mechanical marvels.

Bill took a deep, calming breath before consulting the green and white striped computer print-out that was clutched in his hand. "The what is the Cove Book Shop in Camden Cove, Virginia. The who is the proprietor, one Abigail F. Wetherby."

"And what has dear Abigail done?"

"For the past two months she has been sabotaging *my* entire billing system, that's what she's done!" Bill blurted angrily.

Dominick arched a dark brow. "I thought *our* system was infallible." He glanced over at Ann, noting with satisfaction that she had slid into a gold side chair and began taking notes.

Bill exhaled between clenched teeth. "Look, Mr. Bennett, I realize only too well that many people, yourself included, look upon computer technology as pure dehumanization. It's not as though we've re-created Frankenstein's monster here at Charge-X. As a matter of fact, we have streamlined the entire system so that our customers benefit on all levels. All we ask them to do is cooperate with our system. We've even provided a special kit that makes their job almost effortless."

Dominick had to agree. Over a year ago, when his father had first installed the data processing tools, the entire system had only enhanced corporate productivity and effectiveness for all who had joined Charge-X. "What exactly has happened?"

11

"It started about eight weeks ago when we sent out the new purchase and credit kits to all our customers. All they had to do was use the special lead pencils that were provided and send back the two computer cards twice a month with their receipts. The pre-punched cards are then loaded into the reader and processed," Bill explained authoritatively. "The cards should have been processed smoothly. Instead, the reader jammed, sending mangled data cards all over the room. We spent an entire day repunching and manually redoing all the cards. Two weeks later, the same problem occurred."

"Could the new credit kits have been at fault?" Dominick inquired.

"That's the first thing I thought of. I quickly had new kits sent special delivery," Bill reported. "That didn't stop the jamming. I even had the reader inspected and cleaned. The jamming still continued. I wasted a lot of my, uh, your valuable time trying to solve this mystery. This month I personally checked the cards before putting them into the reader. They all appeared normal and none of the cards seemed damaged externally. They were all doing just fine—until the machine hit Miss Wetherby's card," he stated emphatically.

"I'm not quite sure I understand." Dominick frowned.

"Somehow, she added extra punches to her computer card. The sensitive reader literally balked at accepting the strange codes and jammed the entire system. It was something none of us ever thought to look for. You should see the card room! Before we could stop the machine, it had shredded and ejected cards all over!"

Dominick tried, albeit unsuccessfully, to stifle an appreciative grin. He had never really liked the sudden proliferation of computers in American life. They were everywhere, a mechanical invasion force that raided department stores, restaurants, grocery stores, subway stations, and business offices. The latest craze was having a computer terminal in your own home. With that many computers in operation, snafus were being widely reported. Man versus machine was a frustrating reality. He turned to Ann, but was surprised to find she had surreptitiously left the office.

"Bill, I sympathize with your problem. I can appreciate the number of man-hours it takes to assimilate all that destroyed data. Have you contacted Miss Wetherby to find out why she's been repunching our cards?"

"Mr. Bennett, I deal with machines. I'm not even sure I like dealing with people, and if I ever got my hands on Miss Wetherby—" he stammered angrily, his fingers curling with repressed hostility. "I realize all this must seem extremely humorous to you," he continued stonily, noting Dominick's wry expression. "It's quite true that machines make errors and they are only as good as their programmers. You are fortunate enough to have the best computer programming department in the business. All my staff are quality trained technicians."

"I've no doubts that your department is—" Dominick started, only to have his compliment waved aside.

"Despite the few problems, most people welcome the benefits of automated and computerized equipment," Bill York said stiffly, his entire manner seeming to be one of chastisement. "We've extended credit-card verification and loan applications around the clock. Computerized management saves millions of dollars every year. All we ask for is minimal customer cooperation!"

"Damn it! You're right Bill!" Dominick slammed the palm of his hand on the top of his desk. "We can't let one account ruin a model of electronic perfection. Charge-X will show this Wetherby woman that the computer is mightier than the human," he continued in a voice roughened by his ill health rather than anger. "Don't worry about it. I'll handle this personally. We could ruin that bookshop with a bad credit rating just on her sloppy reporting practices alone."

"Well, thank you, Mr. Bennett," Bill stammered eagerly. "I'm glad you're finally seeing it from our standpoint." He handed Dominick the file and left the office feeling extremely pleased with his boss's improved outlook on computer power.

"What a lot of horse manure that was!" Ann commented dryly, striding in from her own private office.

"You know it and I know it, but that's what York wanted to hear." Dominick grinned unrepentently. "Where did you disappear to?"

"I bypassed all the machines and went to our growing miscellaneous file on a hunch," Ann told him, spreading open a folder in the center of his desk.

14

"It seems that Miss Wetherby has been trying to cancel her store's Charge-X account. She's written five letters advising us that she is no longer accepting any credit cards at her shop and will not waste her valuable time completing our forms. By discontinuing credit cards, she can give her customers cash discounts and let them use an in-house lay-a-way plan."

Dominick leafed through the collection of typed letters, noting that they had started out with a friendly request for cancellation and progressively become more defensive as her requests were never acknowledged.

"Why wasn't all this channeled to the proper department?" he grated hoarsely, looking up from the papers with displeasure.

"The problem is with our system," Ann explained, settling her hip on the corner of his desk. "We can extend or recall credit accounts at will, but we don't seem to have the facilities to accommodate any business that wishes to cancel us. As a matter of fact, as far as I or anyone can determine, this is the first time Charge-X has ever been canceled."

"I understand quite a few gasoline retailers have canceled bank credit cards, but Charge-X deals only with retail trade merchants and a select few at that. I wonder why—" The intercom buzzer interrupted Dominick's musings.

Ann listened to her secretary, punched the hold button, and rolled her hazel eyes expressively. "It's Miss Reynolds, for the fourth time today," she commented dryly.

15

Dominick groaned. "I suppose I can't keep putting her off forever." He rubbed his forehead with his left hand and extended his right for the receiver.

"Hello, Marie," he said tersely, watching Ann glide out of his office with a wry expression on her face.

"I've been trying to catch up with you all day!" came a rather explosive, high-pitched whine. "Really, Dominick, you could be more considerate."

"Well, you've got me now, what's the problem?"

"I just wanted to remind you about the dinner party I'm giving tomorrow night and the art council's ball on Saturday." Her voice had taken on its usual seductive quality that Dominick had come to know so well. In his mind the image of her model-thin body, clad in an expensive negligee and her blond hair arranged in some casual style—managed only by hours with her beautician—achieved startling clarity.

"Look, Marie, I'm really under the weather with this damn cold. I don't think I'll be able to make either affair."

"Dom-i-nick." She made three syllables out of his name. "You must come, darling. I've promised everyone you would. After all, it's not every day they get to meet a famous author who's also the president of such a prosperous company."

He could just envision the childish moue forming on her exquisite face. Dominick ran a hand around the collar of his pale blue linen shirt and pulled out the knot of his gray silk tie. He must be sicker than he thought because lately the sexy, very available

16

Marie Reynolds was leaving a bad taste in his mouth. Her constant need for being the center of attention and her own self-serving greed had left him with the distinct impression of being used. He instantly recalled the adverse effects such relationships had on his father.

"Marie, I'm really sorry," he stated firmly, "but the answer is no. As a matter of fact, I'm going out of town."

"Out of town!" The shrill tone was back in her voice and grated harshly in his ear. "You just said you were ill and now you have the gall to tell me you're going on some . . . some . . . business trip!"

"I didn't say it was business. Actually, it's for health reasons." *Mental health,* he amended silently.

"Listen to me, Dominick Bennett," Marie hissed, "you just can't stand me up like this. Nobody ever has and—"

"Well, there's a first time for everything, Marie. I've really got to go." He quickly slid the receiver back on the phone, cutting off her vituperative expletives.

Dominick stared in silent contemplation at the elaborate design on the acoustical ceiling. The tiles were as complex as his own life had become this past year. He was being forced into the role of company president when all he wanted to do was write.

Initially, he had succumbed to the seduction of corporate politics. Charge-X was financially stronger and more successful than ever. He had reaped the rewards of money, power, and women; but he was beginning to tire of the game, resent the people, and he found himself growing angry and restless with self-disgust. He needed a way out.

Something snapped in Dominick. He pushed himself out of the president's chair and pressed the buzzer for Ann.

"Bill York just gave me a lecture on the merits of automation enhancing corporate effectiveness this afternoon," Dominick told her. "You've been lecturing me on taking sick leave. Well, I've decided you're both right."

"Both?" She eyed his tall, pacing figure with perplexity.

"That's right," he smiled pleasantly. "I'm leaving the entire company on electronic power and taking the two weeks' vacation due me this year, the twenty days' sick leave all employees are entitled to, and the one week personal time that is also listed in the company benefits booklet."

"You've just eliminated the entire month of July," Ann pointed out wryly.

"So I have," Dominick grinned. He removed his gray suit jacket and unbuttoned his shirt collar, feeling his spirits soar with impending freedom. "I know and you know that you can handle any problems that come up at this end. York claims his machines can handle their end and I am going to handle my end."

"Which is?"

"I'm going to take my typewriter out of mothballs, dust off the half-completed novel I put away last year, kill off Dominick Bennett, and resurrect Nick Maxwell, author." He gave her a mock bow.

"Bravo!" Ann clapped her hands with approval.

"If anything should come up, where will you be, at home?"

He frowned. "Staying in New York will not help. I've really got to get away, relax, get rid of this flu bug and get back into the writing life." His eyes fell to the file folder on his desk. "Camden Cove."

"Camden Cove?" she echoed, a puzzled frown creasing her forehead.

"That's right," he nodded enthusiastically. "It sounds like the perfect sleepy, seaside resort where one could rent a cottage and step back into reality. We also owe one Abigail Wetherby an apology so she'll stop jamming our computers."

Ann laughed. "Listen, anyone who can successfully jam up a million dollars' worth of machinery deserves a prize!"

Dominick headed for the door. "I'll let you know where I settle. You could always get in touch with my father, the old fraud, and tell him to get back to work. I think he's exhausted his company benefits!"

He paused, turning back for one final farewell look at the plush designer office that had been his cell for the past year. The telephone rang. Ann picked it up, grinned at him and said in a firm voice: "I'm sorry, Dominick Bennett is on vacation, may I help you?"

CHAPTER TWO

"Nick" 's first impression of the Cove Bookshop brought the word *quaint* to mind. It was a rambling, three-story Victorian house at one end of the small seacoast town. The interior walls had been removed to provide open displays of paperback books on the first level, hardcover volumes on the second level, with paintings by local artists decorating a gallery-type open balcony.

He had spent the better part of an hour choosing a selection of reference books and studying the shop's two proprietresses.

One was a petite, slender ash blonde still in her early teens who, he had heard, was called Dee. She was busy restocking the children's section on the lower level and seemed to have a natural rapport with the few customers who had wandered in during the morning.

The other woman Nick assumed was Abigail Wetherby and, apparently, Dee's mother. She was also an attractive, small-boned woman in her early fifties with short-cropped beige hair and an affable manner. Hardly the type to sabotage a computer!

Nick collected his books and wandered down the curved wrought-iron staircase to the checkout counter.

"Well, you're certainly giving our Saturday morning sales a boost." The woman smiled at him. "That totals forty-five dollars."

He returned the smile and reached for his leather wallet. Hesitating for a moment, he handed her a two-by-three white and orange striped plastic card.

Her smile faded. "I'm sorry. We no longer accept charge cards." She spoke the words slowly, trying to keep a pleasant quality in her tone.

"You've got the decals on the window," Nick pointed out smoothly.

"I realize that but—"

"You also don't seem to have any other notices on display for your customers," he persisted.

"What's the problem, Mom?" Dee asked, watching the dark-haired stranger with undisguised interest.

"This gentleman wants to use his Charge-X card," her mother explained quietly. "He's most insistent."

"We'd better ring for Abby," Dee whispered quickly. "She'll hit the roof if you take a credit card, especially that one," she hissed, before turning a charming smile in Nick's direction. "If you wait just

21

a moment the owner of the shop will be right with you."

Nick was momentarily disconcerted. Apparently, he had yet to meet Abigail Wetherby!

The call buzzer halted Abby's wrestling match with a forty-pound carton of book returns that refused to be pushed into an out of the way corner. She scrambled up off all fours, wiped dusty hands on her green smock, and climbed the cellar stairs to the main level of the store.

"What's up, Mom?" she asked, her hand leaving a dirt smudge on her cheek as she impatiently brushed aside a fallen brown curl.

"Abby," her mother swallowed hesitantly, "this customer would like to *charge* his purchases."

Abby's slate gray eyes gave full attention to the man leaning indolently against the counter. She watched him straighten and leave a bookmark display to move closer to the cash register. She judged him to be a few inches over six feet. His broad shoulders and muscular physique were emphasized by his close-fitting mustard golf shirt and tan slacks. His thick dark brown hair and eyes accented his ruggedly handsome face.

"Excuse me, sir. I'm afraid we no longer accept any type of credit cards in this shop," Abby told him firmly, giving the stranger a slight professional smile.

"You haven't any signs posted," Nick repeated pleasantly.

She frowned and looked over the top of the register to the counter below. "We did . . ."

"It fell behind the counter, Abby," Dee interjected sheepishly before repositioning a flower-decorated notice on top of the old crank-type cash register.

Seeing the stranger's wry smile, Abby took a deep breath. "All the same, I am sorry. We don't accept credit," she stated again tersely.

"I have quite a large order," Nick drawled significantly, his brown eyes appraising her frankly. She was more than a head taller than both her mother and sister, with long brown hair escaping in thick curly tendrils from an untidy topknot. Cool gray eyes dominated the strong, attractive features of her softly rounded face.

Abby flushed under his intense gaze and hurriedly glanced at the stack of books on the counter, mentally tabulating his bill. Since she had taken over sole ownership of the bookshop six months ago, keeping it a profitable moneymaking venture was her primary concern.

The sight of the small plastic charge plate turned her gray eyes into chips of steel. "I've canceled all dealings with the credit companies, especially Charge-X. It's run by an absolute incompetent!" she stated brusquely. "I'll be glad to take a check, even an out-of-state one. I'll even lose the sale." Her rigidly set shoulders and icy voice allowed no further compromise.

"I'm not an out-of-towner," Nick said slowly, watching the play of emotions cross her face. There was a distant look in her eyes that intrigued him, femininity lost beneath a mask of efficiency. For some inexplicable reason he had to fight the urge to reach out and wipe the smudge of dust off her cheek.

"I'm sorry," Dee interrupted quickly, "we know most of the people in the Cove."

"I've just taken Gull Cottage for the month," Nick informed her, his eyes still focused on her sister.

"That makes you our next-door neighbor!" Dee exclaimed excitedly. "He can open a store account, can't he Abby?"

Abby was momentarily discomforted to find her breathing a bit labored over this news and pulled her eyes hastily away from Nick's compelling gaze. "Yes." She swallowed convulsively. "Yes, of course." She reached under the counter into a mesh basket, passing him the proper form and a pen.

Nick's bold writing quickly filled the page. "That's everything except for the telephone number, which escapes my memory."

"That's okay," Dee grinned engagingly, eagerly picking up the questionnaire. "We can just shout for you Mr. . . . Maxwell."

He laughed. "You seem to have the advantage on me with the introductions."

"I'm Claire Wetherby," the older woman smiled warmly. "The bubbly one is my daughter Dee and this is my daughter Abby, who owns the store."

"I buy a lot of books, so I'll probably be haunting the shop once I get settled," Nick informed them, taking possession of the gaily flowered plastic bag that contained his purchases and sliding the totally ignored Charge-X card into his breast pocket. "Have a nice day, ladies."

"Isn't he a dream!" Dee gushed, as the door banged closed behind Nick's broad back. "Imagine, he'll be right next door to us for a whole month."

Abby winked at her mother. "I thought Rod Winters made your heart pound this week," she asked innocently, her normal humor returning now that the stranger had departed.

"I wasn't thinking about me," her sister smiled, her blue eyes dancing mischievously in her impish face.

"Dee!" Claire warned her younger daughter hastily, noting the disapproving look settling on Abby's face.

"I think Abby could use a healthy shift of interest from the store," Dee went on, totally oblivious to her sister's darkening features. "After all, Abby's going to be a quarter of a century old at the end of the month. She can't remain celibate forever."

"For heaven's sake, Dee," her mother gasped sharply.

Abby calmly counted to ten while she removed her smock. "I refuse to be dragged into another discussion on my lack of male companions. It is my choice and will remain my choice," she stated in a cold voice that allowed no further discussion. "Now, if you two will take over again for a while, I've got a hairdresser's appointment."

Nick stretched his lengthy frame out on the beach blanket, watching the handful of bathers play tag in the late afternoon surf. Six cottages shared the rock-ridged swimming area at this section of the Cove, and Nick thoroughly enjoyed the privacy and seclusion from the public beach and bathers that Gull Cottage offered. He gave a relaxed sigh, letting the sun bake out the last vestiges of his cold while he mentally congratulated himself on his brilliant decision three days ago to leave corporate politics behind. He had not felt this peaceful and carefree in a long time.

"Hello, Mr. Maxwell. Mind if I join you?"

Nick squinted against the hammering sun and encountered Dee Wetherby's smiling face, her slim boyish figure clad in a brief turquoise bikini. "Please do," he told her, sitting up and offering her a portion of the blanket as sanctuary against the hot white sand. "And call me Nick."

She dimpled engagingly, settling herself close to his side. "You were really fortunate to get this cottage, especially so late in the season. It's the nicest in Camden. Abby calls it a blend of rustic luxury."

Nick laughed. "I was lucky. The couple who rented it ran into problems affording gasoline money to make it here from California," he explained. "The rental agent told me they got no farther than the Grand Canyon before their vacation money ran out."

Dee grimaced. "I guess Abby's right when she says the country seems to be falling apart. No gas, no oil, food prices out of sight, and double-digit inflation."

"That sounds rather pessimistic."

"Well, I guess she has good reason," she muttered vaguely, then continued hastily. "Being in business,

Abby keeps tabs on everything. She really enjoys working, in fact this is the first year she hasn't had two jobs."

Nick raised a quizzical brow. "Sounds a little mercenary to me," he commented, trying to draw out more information about the woman who had so intrigued him yesterday.

"No," Dee shook her head. "In fact, I really believe Abby hates money. I know she hates credit cards." She grinned impishly at him. Suddenly she realized she was talking far too much, when her real mission was to learn more about her handsome companion. Dee flashed Nick her most dazzling smile. "How do you like the Cove so far?"

"It's very quiet, very relaxed, and very restful," he answered dryly, noting her abrupt change in tactics.

"We get a lot of artists here for the summer months," she continued, hoping he'd tell her his occupation. "In fact, Abby puts a lot of paintings on display at the shop."

"I noticed them yesterday. Some were quite good," he agreed.

"Being at the southernmost tip of the Tidewater Basin, they certainly have enough beautiful scenery to paint and interesting historical facts to write about," Dee told him.

"Is Camden Cove big on historical happenings?" he queried, always interested in gathering information for future reference.

"Well, I'm not really into local history," she grinned. "You really should talk to Abby. She's very involved with the historical society." Dee turned her eyes toward the rolling whitecaps and gave an enthusiastic wave. "Here she comes now."

Nick's gaze followed his companion's point of direction. His eyes and body riveted on Abby's tall, golden figure as it emerged from the foaming surf. Her metallic copper-toned maillot was plastered to her lithe body, revealing a rounded, curving figure that yesterday's shapeless work smock had cunningly concealed. Nick muttered hoarsely under his breath.

Dee glanced at him in surprise, quickly hiding a tiny smile of pleasure. Things definitely looked promising, she thought gleefully.

Abby shook the water from her head of newly cropped brown curls. At the sound of her name being called she shaded her eyes and caught Dee's beckoning gesture and the sight of their new neighbor. For some unexplained reason Nick Maxwell's name and face had been haunting her all night. She hadn't had a man intrude on her thoughts in four years and she really had hoped to avoid any further contact with this particular man. Thanks to her younger sister's manipulations, it looked as though that was going to be impossible. Abby had no choice but to join them, perversely declining to share Nick's beach towel in favor of sitting on the hot, white sand.

"Nick's interested in learning about our local history," Dee reported with considerable enthusiasm.

Abby arched a fair brow at her sister's free use of their neighbor's first name. "The historical society is open every day except Sunday, Mr. Maxwell. The fee is just one dollar and it is within walking distance of your cottage," came her clipped reply.

Dee pursed her lips and rolled her eyes heavenward. Honestly, she thought irritably, she'd love to drop a bomb on Abby! "Nick was also interested in some of the paintings you've got on display," she persisted, anxiously trying to set the conversation flowing.

"A few were quite striking," Nick commented lazily, his half-hooded gaze roaming slowly from Abby's slightly averted profile, skipping down to her long, slender legs to finally rest on the rounded curves of her full breasts that the wet maillot revealed with tantalizing near-transparency.

"I change them every month. If you really are interested in a particular painting, you should buy it soon," Abby replied with curt formality. She was beginning to find it increasingly difficult to ignore the masculine body sprawled on the towel. Nick was a handsome man. His face bordered on the rugged side with its carved features, firmly molded mouth, strong jaw, and deeply cleft chin. His muscular arms and chest were covered by a mat of dark curly hair that veed down his flat stomach before disappearing into a pair of close-fitting white swim trunks. His strong thighs and legs were dangerously close to her own body, making her uncomfortably aware of his almost primitive masculine charm.

"I'll have to make sure I come in and pick the one I want." He smiled easily, noting the soft flush of color that began to compete with the tan of Abby's cheeks.

"I should really see if Mom needs any help with dinner," Dee interrupted gaily. "Now you just sit and relax, Abby. I'll call when it's ready." She quickly left them with a cheery wave.

Abby let out an exasperated sigh as she watched Dee run up a sand cliff to the back steps of their beachside cottage. "My younger sister is about as subtle as a sledgehammer. I'm sorry," Abby apologized.

"I'm not. I find your reserve a most intriguing challenge."

"I assure you it's quite unintentional!" she snapped rudely, curling her long legs under her in a protective gesture. She knew she should have gotten to her feet and stalked back to her house, but somehow she felt strangely lightheaded. It's just the sun, Abby scolded her psyche quickly. The sun and the sea. It had nothing to do with her companion. Nothing at all.

"Neither you nor your sister have an accent," he probed idly, watching as she trickled grains of white sand through her fingers. "I gather you're not native Virginians."

"No, we're not natives."

"I bet I can guess which state you originally hail from after forty-nine other questions."

She tried unsuccessfully to hide a smile and caught his answering grin. "Illinois."

"If I start with the first letter of the alphabet and run through all the cities—"

"Chicago," she snapped, no longer amused at his

continued inquisitiveness. It was becoming uncomfortably annoying.

"I see. How did you happen to land in a little place like Camden Cove?"

"Say, what is this," Abby turned on him angrily. "You sound like a nosy news reporter—" She stopped. Now she remembered why his name and face seemed vaguely familiar. She had seen it connected with the newspapers and on a book jacket. *Fall from Olympus.* You're that Nick Maxwell."

He looked surprised. "You have a good memory. That book was published almost two years ago."

"I reviewed your book for the *Cove Journal,*" she returned evenly.

"Am I going to have to make a trip to the newspaper morgue or are you going to tell me your opinion?" Nick smiled tolerantly.

Abby deliberately took her time before answering. "It got the review it deserved."

He laughed and shifted his body on the blanket, causing his arm to brush against her side.

An imperceptible tightening and strain fell over her nerves and she quickly moved away. Nick seemed to be closing in on her. His wit and natural friendliness were disarming and incredibly fascinating. The hot sun and coconut tanning lotion he had applied blended into an intoxicating aroma that dangerously excited Abby's already heightened senses.

To cover her confusion, she picked up a pair of sunglasses Dee had left behind.

"Don't," Nick commanded softly, reaching for her hand as she tried to put the glasses in place. "I

31

like to see people's eyes when I talk to them. You have very beautiful eyes, Abby," he murmured huskily, capturing her chin in his fingers. "There's something else that's different today. Your hair."

"I—I got it cut yesterday," she stammered, unknowingly provocative as she licked her full lips nervously. She could feel the color again searing her cheeks.

"I like it," he told her, fingering one of the many soft curls that framed her face. "It shows off your beautiful bone structure."

A cold mask slid into place over her previously animated features. She jerked her head out of his grasp. "You've quite a way with words, Mr. Maxwell," she said icily. "I'm sure you would have better luck trying them on someone more receptive or putting them on a piece of paper." She lunged to her feet, gathered the few items Dee had left behind, and stalked back to the secure haven of her cottage.

CHAPTER THREE

"I can't see them at all," Dee groaned disgustedly, parting the red-and-white checked Cape Cod curtains on the kitchen window which overlooked the beach.

"If you don't watch out, you're going to fall into the dishwater," her mother warned dryly, putting a bowl of tossed salad on the table. "We really should call Abby. Dinner will dry out."

"Don't you dare!" Dee squealed, turning from the counter. "I cleverly left her with the most exciting man we've had around here in ages and you're worried about her being late for roast chicken."

Claire laughed and shook her head. "Listen, Dee, you'd better stop this matchmaking nonsense. Abby's been taking it pretty well lately, but I don't know how long that temper of hers will stay in check," she warned seriously.

"Honestly, Mom, Abby is just plain stubborn," Dee grumbled, filling three tall glasses with cold lemonade. "All she ever does is work. It's just not normal."

"She's very determined to make a go of the bookshop for all our sakes," Claire reprimanded sternly.

"I can appreciate that," Dee conceded a little self-consciously, thinking of all Abby had done over the years. "That's why I've been hounding her lately. It's time she had a little fun. I'd be glad to work more in the bookshop, just to give her some free time."

"I'll agree with you there. Abby certainly deserves to think more about herself and less about the shop and us too." Her mother sighed thoughtfully.

"A lot of single guys come into the shop, take one look at Abby, and ask her out. But she gives them the cold shoulder." Dee made a little clucking sound with her tongue. "Do you think I'll ever have a figure like hers?" she asked, looking wistfully down at her own just-blossoming body.

Claire momentarily blinked in confusion, then chuckled. "Keep eating all your fruits and vegetables like a good little girl and—"

"You told me that I'd get curly hair like my sister's if I ate all my breadcrusts and that never happened," she interrupted, giving her straight hair a light tug.

"Give yourself time, honey, you're only sixteen."

"I suppose so. But I have the feeling I'm going to have to swallow two grapefruits whole and hope they end up in the right spots if I ever want to look like my sister." She grinned wryly. Dee set the lemonade

34

pitcher on the table and went back to peer out the window. "Nick certainly noticed her figure. Of course, I don't think Abby realizes what happens to her modest little maillot when it becomes wet, but, oh boy, Nick certainly noticed. You should have heard what he said when he saw her come out of the ocean with her new suit plastered to her body," Dee related gleefully.

"Oh? What did he say," Claire inquired with interest, crossing over to share her daughter's view of the beach.

"I don't think Nick realized he even said it out loud."

"Dee!"

"Okay," she laughed. "Nick snapped to attention and stared, then mumbled: 'Aphrodite rising from the sea.' "

"Really?" her mother mused thoughtfully.

"Yes, really. I think it's most poetic." Dee sighed dreamily.

"He's a writer, Dee. He's paid to be poetic," intoned an annoyed voice from the doorway. They both jumped guiltily when they saw Abby, clad in a yellow terry shorts outfit, eyeing them with obvious displeasure.

"We didn't hear you come in," her mother stammered. "Dinner's ready."

"So I noticed," Abby replied tersely. She pulled out a white Bentwood chair and seated herself in her usual place at the head of the table.

"You didn't have to come home so darn quick," Dee grumbled defensively, avoiding her sister's icy glare. She sat down and fingered her red placemat. "You could have talked with him for a while, given him a little encouragement."

"I know, Dee," Abby said sarcastically, shaking out her paper napkin. "If it was up to you, we'd be making love on the beach right now."

"Would that be so terrible?" Dee shot back. "The man is gorgeous!"

"I'm a throwback. I just don't happen to think a relationship that is based solely on sex and physical attraction is headed anywhere."

"Then you do admit you're attracted to him." Dee pounced on her sister's statement eagerly.

"That's just about enough!" Claire interjected quickly, noting the thunderous look on Abby's face. "I will not have any more of this nonsense. Now eat!" she ordered, slamming the platter of chicken and potatoes on the table. "I want to digest my dinner not get indigestion."

"You know, Mom," Dee commented innocently later, as the three of them were doing the dinner dishes, "it's really a shame that we're the only ones who get to taste your great cooking."

"Did you want to ask one of your friends over for supper?" Claire asked, putting the glassware in the cupboard.

"I was thinking it would be a nice, neighborly gesture if we asked Nick over one night. I'm sure a bachelor would really appreciate a home-cooked meal," Dee continued, carefully avoiding her sister's eyes. "What type of books does he write anyway?" she asked suddenly.

Abby counted to ten, exhaled, and tried not to choke her younger sister with the dishtowel. "I reviewed his last work. It was one of those epoch suspense novels."

"I bet he's as exciting as one of his books," Dee fantasized, instantly visualizing Nick in all sorts of James Bondian situations.

Abby shook her head ruefully at her mother. "He probably rented the cottage to have a little peace and quiet to work on another novel. I doubt he'd appreciate any interruptions, even ones for food."

"I bet he wouldn't mind if you interrupted him, Abby. I could tell by just the way he looked at you this afternoon. He—"

"For heaven's sake," Abby shouted, her controlled reserve slipping. "Would you please stop! I don't need any help from a sixteen-year-old child."

"Well, you aren't doing such a great job on your own," Dee returned heatedly. "You're turning into a female eunich!"

"Do you hear your daughter?" Abby spluttered to her mother. "Where are you getting all this from?"

"I read a lot." Dee's lips twisted sulkily.

"Wonderful," Abby snapped irritably.

"We live in a two-by-two society, you know," Dee went on defiantly. "You just aren't acting normal."

"I'm not normal!" Abby stammered. "You take one lousy high school psych course and think you're Sigmund Freud! Maybe I just like things the way they are. Very uncomplicated, very orderly and—"

"Very boring," her sister finished firmly.

"I am very happy with the boredom," Abby returned in an uncharacteristically high voice that bordered on hysteria. Her chest was heaving with suppressed emotion. She looked from her sister to her mother with anguish-filled eyes that betrayed her feelings more eloquently than she imagined. Abby wadded up the striped dishtowel she was holding and threw it against the kitchen counter before stalking out of the cottage.

"You really should have a little talk with Abby, Mom. I think she has too many unromantic economic issues to deal with," Dee mused thoughtfully, circling the fourth finger of her left hand in a ring of soapsuds.

"I think it's you I'd better have the talk with," Claire replied in a voice that caused Dee to look up at her mother with considerable alarm. "Abby has shouldered a tremendous amount of responsibility over the last four years. I had a hard time adjusting to everything that happened and I'll never have a clear conscience over what happened to Abby." Claire placed an arm around her youngest daughter and hugged her close. "Abby never wanted me to tell you all the facts. She wanted you to have an uncomplicated adolescence, a freedom of mind. I think it's time for you to share a part of your sister's life. Maybe then you'll understand all that Abby has gone through and why she's the way she is."

Dusk was the part of night Abby hated the most. Half dark, half light. A murky gray suspension of time that ironically complemented her life. Abby sat on the cool sand, chin on her updrawn knees, watching the new gently lapping waves play a slow game of tag with the shore.

A brisk run had dissolved her indignant fury. It was hard to stay angry at Dee. She meant well and, in this instance, was annoyingly but absolutely right. Abby had pushed aside all forms of personal pleasure and had become a female eunich—a cold, sterile, sexless automaton that lived solely for work. She hadn't always been like that. There was a time when her life had been full of parties and laughter and men. Abby felt herself drawing away from those thoughts of the past, shrinking within herself, and she silently cursed the chain of events that had changed her life, broken her spirit.

Impatiently, she brushed a hand across wet eyelids. Broken—that wasn't true; dented would be a better word. Lately, she'd been thinking of ending her social and emotional self-imposed isolation. It was seeing Dee blossoming and dating that caused Abby to admit to a natural envy over her younger sister's carefree existence.

They said it was never too late to change, whoever *they* were, she thought wryly. Maybe it was time for her to change, for her to smooth out the dents, do a little body and mind work, make her twenty-fifth year on earth a real birthday. A true new beginning. Subconsciously she had taken a very big first step—cutting her hair, snipping off ten inches of old hair. Abby ruffled her short, fresh curls reflectively. If only it were that easy to snip off old habits, old memories, old nightmares.

She exhaled slowly, scolding herself for her instant

39

loss of confidence. She had proven herself business-wise; now, she had to prove herself social-wise. Maybe she would start by accepting one of those invitations the particularly insistent sports reporter on the *Journal* was always extending, or letting one of the book salesmen take her to lunch. Nothing that could get really complicated; nothing that would get intense. Just a slow, gradual reintroduction into the world of dating. She could handle that, she thought confidently.

Abby stood up, stretched her cramped limbs, and brushed the sand off her legs before slowly wandering back up the beach toward the lights of her cottage.

"Nice night for a walk." A deep masculine voice sliced through the quiet solitude of the night.

"Yes, it is," Abby agreed tensely as Nick Maxwell's broad frame completely blocked her path. She wondered what it was about this man that made her feel so conscious of him every time they met. Why did she feel the need to adopt an unusually rude attitude as a form of self-protection?

"I was hoping I'd run into you again," he continued, studying her face in the gray twilight with keen eyes.

"Oh?"

"I owe you an apology. I had no intention of making you angry this afternoon."

"That's all r-right," she stammered, completely caught off-guard by his statement. Her nerves relaxed under his disarming smile. "I guess I get a little testy on an empty stomach," she said with a sudden flash of humor and restored complaisancy.

Nick's rich laughter echoed over the waves. Abby's face softened into a warm smile, a smile that had remained hidden for a long time.

"I'd like to take another look at those paintings you have on display. What time do you open the shop tomorrow?" Nick asked.

"I'm not open to customers on Mondays," Abby explained. "That's the one day I do my bookkeeping, restocking, and ordering."

"If you let me in, I promise to be very quiet and not disturb you," Nick cajoled in a deep voice that seemed to have a rather unusual effect on her senses. "In fact, I'll even bribe you by bringing lunch. How's that sound?"

"That all depends on what you're bringing for lunch," she parried lightly, marveling at her newfound temerity.

"I'll take that as a definite yes and make sure you're well compensated for this neighborly gesture," he assured her with an amused drawl.

"I'm there by ten and leave the front door unlatched for deliveries so . . ."

"It's a date," Nick replied. "I'll see you tomorrow."

Abby nodded and then bid him a hasty good night, suddenly anxious to get home. A date—her first in four years. Dee would faint!

CHAPTER FOUR

Nick pushed open the door of the bookshop, nearly tripping over a bottle of window spray and a large razor-blade scraper. As he bent to move them aside, the sight of a bloody smear on the window sent an icy chill coursing down his spine.

"Abby!" He shouted her name, dropping the rattan picnic basket he was carrying and running toward the back of the shop.

He found her leaning against the bathroom wall, her left wrist clutched tightly to the front of her light green T-shirt. A T-shirt that was already heavily soaked with blood.

Her ashen face was drawn with pain. "Why is it you can never find a bandage when you need one?" She managed a weak smile, indicating the open medicine cabinet. "I had such a stupid accident."

Nick grabbed her wrist and swore sharply. It

wasn't just a cut, the blood was coming in spurts. He wasted little time, quickly reaching for his clean handkerchief, and pressed it firmly against her wrist. "You've got more than just a cut, lady. You've slashed the artery," Nick stated grimly. Using his free hand, he unhooked and pulled off his belt, quickly lashing it around the handkerchief to form a makeshift pressure bandage that would control the bleeding.

She seemed to go two shades paler under her tan. "I don't think—" Abby stopped, a sudden strong buzzing in her ears causing her to shake her head. That was a big mistake. She momentarily saw black, swayed, and clutched frantically for Nick's shoulder.

"Don't go fainting on me now," he said quickly. His strong arm slipped reassuringly around her waist. "Keep that arm up while I drive you to the hospital," he told her in a calm, steady voice as he half carried her out the front door and into the front seat of his pewter Mercedes.

Abby followed Nick's instructions and kept her arm elevated by balancing her elbow on the black velour door rest. The air-conditioned interior of the powerful car seemed to make it easier for her to breathe, as did Nick's soothing stream of conversation. In a matter of minutes, they reached the nearby emergency beachside clinic. An efficient admissions nurse quickly sized up the situation and immediately led them to a curtained treatment bay where they were joined by Dr. Claymore.

"Abby, I think we're going to have to dedicate a wing to you at this clinic," said the smiling, bald-headed doctor, as he unwrapped Nick's belt and carefully peeled away the red-stained handkerchief. "I've been patching her up since she was a little girl spending summers here with her aunt," he elaborated for Nick's benefit.

"Listen," Abby babbled hopefully, "I'm sure all it needs is a couple of bandages and a little disinfectant. It probably looks worse than it really is."

"No, this really is bad," the doctor said firmly. "You went and sliced across the radial artery. It's going to need stitches."

Abby blanched. She could take pain but there was something about the smell of alcohol and the sight of a needle that caused an acute phobic reaction. "Look, just push the skin together. Super-glue it or something—"

"I wish there were some way of shutting you up, Abby," Dr. Claymore countered dryly. "You are such a lousy patient."

Nick's voice carried over her continual rambling of illogical medical suggestions. "Allow me." He quickly slipped his hand under her chin, lifted her surprised face up to his and put his mouth firmly over hers.

Abby never even felt the local injection of xylocaine the doctor gave her. She did, however, take note that the spinning sensation had returned to her head and her heart had accelerated at an alarming rate.

"That's a very interesting technique you've got there," Dr. Claymore grinned. "You did a great job with the pressure bandage, too, Mr.—"

44

"Maxwell, Nick Maxwell," Nick returned pleasantly, watching with satisfaction as color replaced the unnatural pale of their now docile patient.

Abby sat in a quiet, bemused state while the doctor expertly put ten sutures in her wrist and deftly bandaged her wound.

"That's the best she's ever been," the doctor told Nick with a broad smile, after giving Abby a tetanus booster. "Now look, Abby. That local anesthetic is going to wear off in half an hour and that wrist is going to be mighty sore. I want you to go home and rest. And no work tomorrow, either." His voice overrode her protest. "Listen, you split those sutures carrying boxes of books and I'll have you strapped to a gurney till that wrist heals. Let Dee and your mother take care of you for a change. I'm going to call them—"

"They went to Norfolk for the day," Abby interjected lamely. She suddenly felt very helpless and weary.

"Don't worry, doctor, I'll make sure she follows your instructions," Nick stated firmly.

"I bet you will." Dr. Claymore grinned and handed him an envelope of pills. "Make sure she takes two of these and rests. She's stubborn about taking medication and resting too."

"This is really silly. I could just as easily rest at home," Abby grumbled exasperatedly as Nick all but dragged her out of his car and into the air-conditioned comfort of his house. Gull Cottage was one of the more elegant beach rentals, with richly paneled walls, plush carpeting, and attractive blue and green furnishings.

"Knowing you," he intoned dryly, "you'd probably clean cabinets or scrub a floor. Now march into the bedroom and let me get those blood-stained clothes off you."

"What!" she whirled and cannoned into him, wincing as her sore wrist slapped against his muscular chest.

Nick's jaw hardened threateningly. He unceremoniously picked her up and carried her into his bedroom, gently lowering her to sit on the edge of the wide brass bed. "At times your independence is most annoying," he ground out sharply. "There will be no further discussion." His capable hands pulled the stained T-shirt loose from the band of her dark green cotton slacks. "You will do just as you are told." Gently, he eased the shirt over her head and off her arm. He then proceeded to unbutton her slacks and pulled them off her long legs.

Abby stood before him clad only in a lacy beige bra and peach-colored nylon briefs. She could feel her entire body taking on a pink flush as Nick's dark eyes roguishly assessed her curvaceous form.

"You really enjoy being high-handed, don't you," she snapped angrily, her narrowed gray eyes meeting and holding his challengingly.

His mouth twisted into a smile of devilish amusement while his fingers teasingly traced the tanned outline of her swimsuit that was exposed by her low-cut bra.

"Stop it, Nick," Abby gasped in outrage, her right

hand quickly coming up to halt any further exploration. She took a step backward only to find her progress halted by the side of the bed pressing against her shins.

"That copper bathing suit of yours is much more revealing when it's wet than your charming lingerie," he mocked gently.

"Ah, yes," Abby retorted sarcastically. "Aphrodite rising from the sea." She saw with satisfaction that he had the good grace to blush.

"I'll remember your sister's exceptional hearing in the future," he returned evenly, settling his hands on the bare curve of her waist as he pulled her closer.

The nervous quiver Abby's stomach had acquired snaked upward. She shivered, suddenly afraid of the virile magnetism this man seemed to hold for her. "Nick, can't I have a robe or something?" she pleaded in a desperate voice that held a throb of impending tears.

Nick smiled and seemed to take pity on her. He reached for his blue terry bathrobe. "I gather I can now count on your complete cooperation," he said not unkindly, tying the sash around her slim waist. "I'm going to soak these clothes in cold water and get your pills."

Abby settled herself comfortably on the blue Grecian-key design bedspread and waited for his return. It seemed useless to argue with Nick. He was the most self-assured, dynamic man she had come across in a long time; also, one of the most mentally and physically disturbing. Her fingers lightly brushed across her lips as she recalled the burning imprint his

47

mouth had made when he had applied his own brand of bedside manner at the clinic.

"You'd better take these with milk," Nick told her, settling himself on the edge of the bed and handing Abby two pills and a glass. "You didn't have any lunch, and it's not a good idea to take medication on an empty stomach."

"You were in charge of lunch," she reminded him archly and for the first time thought about the bookshop. "I've got to get back to the store," Abby gasped, trying to swing her legs off the bed.

"What!" Nick hastily put the tumbler down and grabbed her shoulders.

"We just ran off and left the place wide open. My purse is there, the cash box, I've got delivery men coming—"

He pushed her firmly back down against the pillows. "Take it easy. I can see you won't get any rest until all that is taken care of. I'll go back and wait for the deliveries and collect your things," he told her calmly, "if you promise to take your pills and rest."

"You'd really do all that?" Her eyes searched his face in puzzlement. "Why? Why should you want to do this? You hardly know me."

Nick took her hand, his fingers lightly tracing the bandages and smiled down into her confused features. Abby couldn't tear her eyes away from his compelling gaze.

"Hardly know you." He looked thoughtful for a moment. "Maybe in the known definition of time, that is true. I do know you're intelligent and witty and have a mercurial personality." His brown eyes suddenly lit up with mischievous delight. "I have a hunch there's a bit of fire and passion hidden away in you."

The mask slid into place again. Abby looked past him, her previously softened features taking on a look of carved stone, her gray eyes cold and unseeing. "If you're looking for a vacation sex partner for a month of fun and games, you've got the wrong girl," she said icily.

Nick's long fingers cupped her chin, forcing her to focus on his smiling face. "That thought never even crossed my mind." His hands slid up the lapels of the terry robe around to the sensitive nape of her neck, pulling her closer. His mouth deliberately took slow possession of her trembling, full lips. Abby's mouth parted invitingly beneath his. She seemed to have little control over her heightened emotions.

He finally lifted his head and reached for the glass of milk on the night table and the envelope of pills. "Now be a good girl, swallow those pills and take a nap," he directed cheerfully before walking out the bedroom door.

An unfamiliar series of scraping noises woke Abby. She thought Nick had returned. Her eyelids struggled open against an invisible weight, her head felt fuzzy, and her mouth seemed filled with cotton. Worst of all was the dull ache and pinching sensation coming from her left wrist.

She became aware that someone was watching her. He was seated back to front on the ladderback desk chair that he had moved closer to the bed. She had never seen him before in her life but, somehow, he looked vaguely familiar.

The stranger was very distinguished looking with lean features, thick silver-streaked hair, a deeply cleft chin, and brown eyes that fairly danced with amusement. She shut her eyes and wondered if he couldn't possibly be a figment of her imagination caused by the pills she had taken.

"Well," the figment said cheerfully, "I see my son's taste in women has greatly improved!"

Abby's eyes opened wider. "You're Nick's father?"

A silver brow arched expressively. "Yes, I am. And you are?"

"I'm Abby Wetherby, Mr. Maxwell," she smiled politely. "Nick didn't mention you were expected this afternoon."

"I just returned from a cruise and thought I'd surprise him," he returned amiably. "Please, call me John."

Abby struggled to sit up, using her good hand for leverage. "Nick should be back soon. He's waiting for some deliveries at my shop for me. I had a little accident this afternoon." She grimaced ruefully, indicating her bandaged wrist.

"Shop?"

"Yes. I own the Cove Bookshop in town," she explained, immediately warming to his congenial manner.

"Ah, I see," John said slowly, as if his mind were assembling the pieces of some private puzzle.

Abby shook her head, wishing she didn't feel quite

so dull and confused. "I'm afraid the codeine pills are clogging up my mental processes," she apologized.

He smiled and patted her arm. "Why don't you go splash some cold water on your face and move around a bit while I fix us a nice pot of coffee."

The back door opened slowly, causing John to look up from the automatic coffee maker he had just switched on. "That purse goes so well with your outfit, Dom, or should I call you Nick?" he intoned dryly, as his son pushed into the room laden with Abby's straw handbag, a green metal cash box, and a rattan picnic hamper.

"Dad!" Nick jumped guiltily. "What the devil are you doing here?"

"Well, as I told your beautful patient," John drawled significantly, "I came to surprise you with a visit."

"Good Lord!" Nick exclaimed sharply, "You didn't tell Abby your name or—"

"She told me that I must be Mr. Maxwell," he interrupted his stammering son with an accusing look. "Only your mother called you Nick."

Nick quickly strode over, closing the louvered hall doors for privacy before confronting his father. "Did you get a chance to stop at the office before you came down here?"

"Yes. Ann told me the whole story. I gather that charming lady I found asleep in your bed is our computer killer."

"That's her," Nick laughed. "She wasn't exactly what I was expecting."

"So I gather," his father commented wryly, settling himself at the butcher-block table. "Why haven't you told her who you are?"

Nick ran a hand around the back of his neck. "I don't know. I suppose I should have right from the beginning. I have a horrible feeling this lie is going to explode in my face one of these days," he said worriedly. "Abby knows me just as Nick Maxwell, author on vacation."

"Have you been able to find out why she has this particular abhorrence to Charge-X?"

"Not yet. To tell you the truth, Dad, I never intended on getting this involved. I just wanted a chance to get away from that damn office, give one Abigail Wetherby an apology, and get to work on my book. But . . ." His mouth twisted wryly. "I was suddenly overcome with the desire to be Mr. Clever and play detective. Well, I outsmarted myself and now I seem committed to this damn deception." Nick looked up, his dark brooding gaze carefully avoiding his father's eyes. "This is one hell of a way to start a relationship."

"Oh?" John proded gently, watching his son with interest.

Nick sighed, rubbing his palms along the sides of his white jeans, while he tried to clearly assess his emotions. "Something happened here. Something I didn't plan on. It's Abby." He looked at his father questioningly. "There's something about her that makes me feel—feel things I never felt before. I suppose I'm not making much sense, am I?"

His father smiled, almost as if a secret had been

shared between them. "I had those same feelings once, a long time ago."

"I don't like fooling her," Nick grumbled. "I hate all the lies. I'm uncomfortable with them and they get in the way." He jammed his hands in the back pockets of his jeans and thrust out his chin belligerently. "You know, this is all your fault."

"My fault?" John's brow arched in surprise.

"That's right," Nick accused, "if you hadn't gone galavanting around the world, pretending to recover from that phony heart attack, I wouldn't be in this position. I'm trapped. I sure as hell can't walk into that bedroom, flash her my suave smile, and say, 'Oh, by the way, I'm the fellow in charge of that son-of-a-bitch of a computer who keeps threatening you and making your life miserable,' " he grated sarcastically.

John rubbed his forehead painfully. "What are you going to do?"

"As of right this minute, I'm resigning and turning over the presidency of Charge-X right back to you. I'm disassociating myself with the company. My conscience will be clear," he rationalized with a self-satisfied smile."

"And you think that's going to solve your problem?" John returned chidingly. "You're still going to have to tell her just who you are and what you represent. The longer you wait, the worse it's going to be to get those words out," he warned his son.

"Don't you think I realize that?" Nick groaned. "I just don't think this is the right time."

"When *is* the right time?"

A slight noise caused Nick to look toward the doorway. A smile settled over his sober features as he caught sight of Abby's tall figure wrapped in his short navy bathrobe hovering uncertainly by the café doors.

She tentatively pushed them open farther, eyeing father and son hesitantly. "I hope I'm not interrupting," she all but stammered.

"Nonsense." John smiled kindly. "You've timed it perfectly, the coffee's just done," he told her, offering her his chair.

Nick settled his lengthy frame in the chair next to hers. "How's the wrist?" he asked, letting his long finger slide down the sensitive vein on the inside of her arm until it encountered the gauze-covered wrist.

Abby wrinkled her nose. "It hurts," she admitted ruefully. "I'm glad you made me rest."

Nick laughed. "That's quite an admission coming from such a determined, stubborn workaholic."

"How the devil did that happen?" John asked, setting three steaming mugs of coffee on the table along with spoons, milk, and sugar.

"It was really the stupidest accident," she recounted, scooping two teaspoons of sugar into her cup. "I just got so mad after I read the morning mail at that stupid Charge-X Company that I took a razor blade and was determined to get their damn decal off my front window!" she told them angrily.

Nick all but choked on a mouthful of black coffee. His father quickly passed him a napkin.

"What did Charge-X send you in the mail?" John hastily interjected, covering for his still gasping son.

54

"That company is run by two idiots—one human, one a machine," Abby told him. "I have been trying to cancel my store account with them for two months. I've written all sorts of letters, but all they do is send me threatening notices about not filling out their stupid forms. So," she confided with obvious relish, "I've had a friend of mine repunch their computer cards."

"Has that solved your problem?" Nick asked, his voice slightly higher than normal, as he brushed off the front of his white knit shirt with another napkin.

"I thought it would," she said dejectedly, "but today I got two letters. One was a printed computer form informing me that if I don't send back their record cards, I stand the risk of damaging my store's credit rating and possible legal action."

"What was the second letter?" John asked uncomfortably.

"That was the frosting on the cake," Abby said indignantly. "It was an invitation from their company president to apply for a personal credit account because of my good business rating." She shook her head with disgust. "Can you believe the nerve of that man Barrett or Bennett? I'm stuck on a merry-go-round with that stupid company and its computer, and there doesn't seem any way to get off."

John exchanged an embarrassed silent glance with Nick. The first chance he got, he vowed mentally, he was calling his office to get Abby's problem solved once and for all.

"Not many businesses cancel credit companies

these days," Nick probed, trying to draw out further details now that the door had been opened.

"Well, they should. Too many people get caught in the tentacles of credit companies and find they can't control the monster," Abby said bitterly, suddenly lowering her eyes and pretending an extreme interest in the intricate wood pattern on the table top.

Any further discussion by John and Nick was abruptly ended by a repeated, agitated knocking on the back door.

"Abby, are you all right?" Claire and Dee cried in unison as they rushed into the room. "We ran into Dr. Claymore at the drugstore and he told us what happened."

"I'm fine," Abby told them with a game smile. "Luckily, Nick knew first aid."

"So Dr. Claymore mentioned," Dee smiled wickedly, her eyes pointedly focused on the bathrobe her sister was wearing. Abby could feel the color surge into her cheeks.

Nick quickly stepped in and introduced his father to Abby's family.

"Well, I'm very thankful you were there, Nick," Claire told him earnestly. "I know just how stubborn my daughter can be when it comes to asking for help. More than likely she probably thought a bandage would suffice."

"That's exactly what I found her looking for," he recounted with a laugh.

"You should see the fuss she put up when she had to have her appendix out two years ago," Dee added with amusement. "She thought a bandage could fix that too."

"Okay, okay," Abby called over their communal laughter. "I'm just a bad patient. I'm sure by tomorrow morning this wrist will be as good as new and I'll be back at work."

"Work! Tomorrow!" Dee gasped. "No way. The doctor said you are to rest for at least a day."

"Well, that would be today," Abby insisted stubbornly.

"That means tomorrow too," her mother interrupted firmly. "I think Dee and I can manage without you for one day."

"But I have today's work to get done too."

"Listen, Abby, if you split those stitches, you are going to have a real problem. The doctor warned me about you," her mother said impatiently. "I know you, you just won't sit quietly and do paperwork."

"Well, I just can't sit around the house and mope," Abby muttered grudgingly, reluctant to give up the battle.

"How about helping me," Nick's voice cut in, causing the three women to remember their male audience with much embarrassment.

"Helping you? How?" Abby inquired curiously.

"Well, I could use a proofreader on the manuscript pages I've typed. You could just relax and carefully read over what I've completed for errors. That certainly won't strain your wrist and I'd be interested in a reviewer's criticism."

Abby looked at him for a long moment then nodded. "All right. I think I'd like that."

John, who had been studying Claire with interest, spoke suddenly. "How about if I help out in the bookshop tomorrow? Neither of you ladies should be lifting heavy books, and I'd enjoy coming out of retirement."

Claire looked at Nick's father and smiled hesitantly. "I think I'd like that too."

CHAPTER FIVE

"What are you giggling about, woman?" Nick said with mock anger, as he pushed himself away from his cluttered desk. "That book is supposed to be high suspense, not humor!"

"It's your typing errors. Some of them are priceless." Abby grinned at him. "My favorite is, and I quote, she murmured bloatedly." Abby puffed out her cheeks, causing Nick to chuckle in amusement.

"Okay, so I am not the world's best typist," he grinned, walking over to the round, glass-topped dining-room table where she was working. "How's your wrist feeling?" he questioned, watching her face for any signs of pain.

Abby wrinkled her nose and stood up to stretch, looking cool and comfortable in a red knit sleeveless top and khaki shorts. "It pinches but it's fine," she shrugged. "I feel a fraud staying out of work."

Nick gave an exasperated sigh and settled his hands heavily on her shoulders, pushing her back into the green velvet upholstered chair. "Even company presidents are allowed sick leave," he told her dryly. "Be a good, quiet girl and I'll fix us lunch after I finish typing the rest of this chapter." He bent his head, brushing his lips lightly across her forehead before returning to his desk.

Abby, however, couldn't go back to correcting the manuscript. Her gray eyes refused to focus on the typewritten pages spread out on the table before her. Instead, they were pulled by some unseen, almost magnetic force back to Nick. Since his back was toward her, Abby was free to study him with unguarded scrutiny.

Her gaze slid slowly over his neatly styled head of vibrant dark hair, across his broad shoulders, their muscles flexing under the thin cotton of his dark green T-shirt as he typed, and finally to his long, sinewy legs revealed by a pair of white tennis shorts. Physically, Nick was a potent package. Intellectually, he was even more dynamic. Abby reluctantly had to admit that against her will she found herself liking this man—liking him a little too much. She had spent the morning correcting his novel and reading between the lines of the story as it unfolded on paper.

She had done enough book reviews to know that even though the plot and characters were fiction, quite a bit of an author's personality and emotions leaked through. She liked the many facets of Nick's personality and felt he could be very understanding. She began to respond quite naturally to his teasing in a way she'd never done before. She felt her defenses slipping away. Nick had added a positive new dimension to her life.

His voice brought her out of her daydreaming with its invitation to follow him into the kitchen. "I'm making BLTs for lunch," Nick told her, as he extracted lettuce, a giant tomato, and a package of bacon from the refrigerator.

"That's one nice thing about being sick—no one expects you to help," Abby smirked complacently at him before giving an exaggerated grimace as he threw the entire pound of bacon into the frying pan.

"I'll put you in charge of toasting the bread." He grinned, snapping the gas stove to life. "How do you like the book so far?"

"I thought the way to a man's heart was by feeding his stomach, not his ego," she teased.

"Are you after my heart, Abby?" Nick looked up from slicing the tomato to stare at her intently.

"That's just a figure of speech," Abby stammered, looking hurriedly down at the toaster controls and away from his probing brown eyes.

"I'll let you off the hook this time," came his lazy rejoiner.

"Can I use the phone?" she asked abruptly, anxious to change the direction their conversation had taken. "I want to call the shop."

"Why?"

"Because I want to check on how things are going, what came in the mail, see if there are any problems," she told him with a puzzled frown creasing her smooth forehead.

61

"Don't you think your mother would have called if there were any problems?" Nick asked evenly, giving the now sizzling pan a shake. "Can't you forget about the bookshop for one day?"

"*My* shop is very important to me. I've got a big responsibility," she said stiffly. "*Your* writing is important to you. Every word has to be perfect."

"That's different. I—"

"Your work is different?" Abby taunted, her voice heavy with sarcasm at his rather patronizing tone. "What a male chauvinist you are! I'm surprised you had the nerve to fry your relative for lunch," she added nastily, indicating the sputtering pan of bacon.

"What are you so angry about?"

"I've skipped anger and gone directly to rage!" she snapped. "I'm really surprised at your attitude. I thought you were more mature than that. I didn't think you were capable of harboring those outmoded, condescending ideas."

"Wait a minute," he interjected. "You're misunderstanding what—"

"You know," she carried on, completely ignoring him, "you've really got a lot of nerve trying to tell me how to run my business, my life, after knowing me for three days."

"Look, I am not trying to tell you what to do," Nick said evenly, hoping to calm her down. "I know you've been working hard. Damn hard. Dee said this is the first year you haven't had two jobs."

Abby tapped her foot in annoyance at her sister's gossip. "I've had to work like that. We needed the money." It was almost a plea.

"I don't understand—"

"You could never understand."

Nick shook his head. "It seems to me, if you needed financial help you could have taken out a loan or gotten credit—"

She gave a bitter, humorless laugh, icelike chips forming in her eyes. "How do you think I ended up in such a mess?"

"Damn it, Abby, sometimes you talk in riddles!" he said exasperatedly. "You act like you have some dark, terrible secret. You'd think you'd murdered someone."

Abby swallowed the bitter lump that threatened to strangle her. She closed her eyes against the pain, fighting the burning tears that she could no longer hold back. Her voice broke into jerky sobs as all the old memories came flooding vividly back into her mind. "That's just the point. I did kill somebody."

Abby's tortured confession was suspended in mid-air, for the splattering bacon grease had teased the gas flame once too often, causing the frying pan to ignite in a flash of revenge. Nick jumped for the stove, quickly snapped off the burner and doused the fire with salt from a nearby canister.

"Abby, what the hell are you talking about?" he asked sharply, his eyes still on the smoldering pan he'd put in the stainless-steel sink. Nick turned for her answer and found she was gone.

In the distance Abby could hear Nick shouting her name. She didn't answer. She tucked her long legs under her, curling her numb body into a protective

63

fetal position, finding comfort and strength in the wet, rocky ledge that provided her with shelter. The pounding whitecaps broke against the jagged cliffs below. Gradually their swelling crescendo replaced the voice calling in the distance, leaving her alone with the infinite surging sea.

She had found the cavelike bunker years ago on one of her summer visits to her Aunt Emily's. Despite its cold roughness and the angry surf below, the ledge had become a womb where she'd often sought refuge while coming to terms with her problems.

Today the sea offered no soothing caresses, no tranquil solace, only another punishing blow to her battered psyche. The peaceful whispers were replaced by the faceless wailings of demons from the past. Abby knew she had been lying to herself. Her life hadn't grown simpler and more controllable, only more complicated. The dead still manipulated the living. Fresh transfigurations of her past burned itself into every moment of today. She had hated so long that her courage and her strength had been reduced to fear. Abby burrowed tighter against the rocks, hoping to absorb their strength to replenish her own.

Over an hour later Nick found her. He had searched her house, called the bookshop on a phony pretext, and then in desperation began to run up and down the beach. He had spotted a flash of red in the jagged cliffs far down the coast and prayed it was Abby's T-shirt.

He was out of breath when he finally reached her, more from fear than physical exertion. "I've been out of my mind looking for you—" He stopped. "You can't make a statement like that then run away." He stopped again, running a hand anxiously over his face.

He took a deep breath and sat down close beside her on the rock ledge, waiting and watching, mentally transmitting his empathy. Finally, his gentle voice broke through her emotional wall. "Tell me about it."

"Why?" Abby's voice was lifeless as she continued to stare down at the foaming waves.

His hand caught her chin, pulling her face toward his. He could see the anguish which was all too apparent in the depths of her gray eyes. "Sometimes you have to take out the past, look at it, then put it away forever," he said, choosing his words carefully.

"I've never let anyone get this close." Her voice faltered.

Nick took her trembling hand in his, letting his strong fingers intertwine with her own. "I need to know you."

Abby stared at him, searching his face for some sign, something that would reassure her. The sudden impact was almost intangible. For some reason she felt she could make Nick understand. She desperately wanted to share her fears and needs with this man. "It's a long, horrible story," she said finally.

Nick slid his other arm around her waist, drawing her closer to his warm body. "We've got all the time in the world."

For a long while Abby simply continued to stare at their entwined fingers, saying nothing, but her mind's painful resurrection of the past was evident on her constricted features. When she finally spoke, it was in a curious, detached voice. "Four years ago we lived in one of Chicago's most fashionable neighborhoods. We had a big Georgian-style mansion, three cars, membership in the best country club—we had the best of everything.

"I had gone to the club that morning to play tennis. My partner sprained her ankle after the first set, abruptly ending our game. I decided to go back home to relax. I knew my mother had gone to a club meeting. Dee was at summer camp and I would have the house and pool all to myself.

"I was surprised to see my father's car in the driveway, especially that early in the day. He seldom managed to make it home until very late most evenings.

"I no sooner walked in the front door when I heard an explosion—a roar of some sort from the den." Abby swallowed and continued with great difficulty. "My father always carried large amounts of money on him and I thought he must have surprised a thief. I must have gone crazy. I grabbed the fireplace poker and went charging into the study like some comic-book heroine. There wasn't any burglar. Only my father—slumped over his desk with half his head missing."

Nick made an involuntary exclamation. He felt sick at the thought of what Abby had witnessed.

She took a deep breath. "The next part is hazy. One of the neighbors heard the shot and my scream —I don't even remember screaming. The next thing

I knew there were sirens, police, an ambulance, and lots of questions. My mother arrived amid all the confusion."

Abby's voice was low, barely squeezing through the lump in her throat. "The verdict was suicide. I just couldn't believe it. I prayed the coroner would find something. I don't know—a brain tumor, cancer —anything. But he didn't. We hunted for a note, we needed a reason. We never found a thing.

"When the news got out, to say all hell broke loose would be an understatement. My father was an investment counselor. The authorities froze everything while they checked the books and files.

"Soon irregularities began to show up and a full-scale investigation was launched. The rumors were rampant about mishandling of funds, missing securities, mismanagment of customer accounts. They were all proven true. My father had overextended his credit and embezzled a small fortune to cover his losses from people who had trusted him with their savings. If that wasn't enough, we found that he owned a condominium that he'd given to another woman—his mistress."

Abby's voice faltered. "I'll never forget the look on my mother's face when the authorities came to us with all this evidence. She was on the verge of a complete mental and physical collapse." Abby was silent for a moment, remembering.

"Mom had only her older sister, Emily, left. She came for the funeral and was an incredible anchor through the entire mess. Between the two of us we convinced Mom to take Dee and come back here to

Camden Cove and live with Aunt Emily. A very close friend of my aunt's was a psychologist. He was able to give Mom the therapy she needed and answer all of Dee's questions."

"What about you?" Nick asked in a voice thick with shared pain.

Abby gave a humorless laugh. "I was twenty-one and convinced I could handle everything. I had lawyers and one person I thought I could really lean on.

"At any rate, the bulk of it was out of my hands. A cold, impersonal court receiver came in and put a price tag on our life. There was no insurance, of course, but the house had appreciated in value. The cars and other property were sold to pay back all the creditors. When it was all finished, I was still left with a sizable pile of personal family debts to pay off. I made arrangements with most of the creditors to pay it off in installments over the next few years."

"You didn't have to do that," Nick interrupted.

"I know, but somehow I had this horrible guilt feeling that it had all been our fault," Abby said fervently. "My father was never the type of man you could get close to. He'd never shared himself with any of us. Consequently, Mom, Dee, and I formed our own tight unit, making him feel even more of an outsider. He'd buy us everything. I never really asked for the car on my birthday, the private schools, the club membership, but I never said no either. Subconsciously I felt it was my fault that the debts piled up. Dee was only twelve, but I should have been able to realize what was happening. Here I was, a business major and I couldn't spot a damn thing. I was in a love-struck fantasy world of my own."

"Was that the one person you thought you could count on?" he asked hesitantly.

Abby nodded. "Eric Dalton," she said in a cold, toneless voice. "I had met Eric at one of the club dances. He was handsome and charming and I was thrilled and flattered that he should be interested in me over all the other beautiful girls. He moved fast and he talked fast. After only a handful of dates he wanted to get engaged. He even suggested we elope. For some reason I kept stalling." She looked at Nick, a puzzled crease marring her smooth forehead. "It's something I can't explain. I could never seem to let myself go with Eric. It was as if some sixth sense was holding me back, making me wary." Her voice trailed off. "Anyway, I later found out it was really my father that interested Eric. Marry the daughter and get in good with the rich old man by playing the dutiful son-in-law. Eric's interest in me was directly related to how prosperous my father's business was.

"But then, I wasn't the only girl Eric had zeroed in on. The other was a dainty blonde. Her father wasn't quite as wealthy, but she was quite pregnant. There was a sickening confrontation among the three of us one morning that I'll never forget. I was devastated. I had lost my father, my home, my mother was lost in her own private mental battle, and now I had lost the man I loved—or thought I loved. All the mistakes kept piling up, showing me just what a failure I had been. I had lost everything, especially my self-esteem." Abby took a deep breath. Her voice

69

seemed tougher than before. "Self-preservation is a powerful force. I had to stand by myself, learn to be strong because everything around me was falling apart. I finished up what I had to do in Chicago, got on a plane, and joined the rest of my family here in Camden.

"I worked with Aunt Emily in her bookshop during the day and at night and on weekends I was a waitress, sending everything to the creditors to pay off the bills."

"My God, you must have been in a state of mental and physical exhaustion yourself," Nick breathed heavily.

"I was grateful for exhaustion," she whispered. "It stopped the nightmares; it stopped the tears from seeing my mother sitting day after day in a rocking chair and staring; it stopped my hearing Dee's constant questions. Exhaustion stops pain." The release of Abby's pent-up emotions allowed her tears to finally run free. "It took my mother over a year to make progress, to begin to care again for herself as well as for the rest of us. She showed a marked improvement when I had my appendix operation. Then Aunt Emily had a massive heart attack. Mom took care of her while I took over control of the bookshop. The medical bills piled up again and I still held down a waitressing job. Even Dee helped with babysitting wages. Just six months ago, dear Aunt Emily died.

"She was very generous, leaving the cottage to Mom and the bookshop to me." Abby sniffed and wiped the wetness from her cheeks with her hand. "I feel this enormous weight of responsibility to make sure this business doesn't fail. Can you understand? Can you possibly understand all the pressures and the feelings I have? All the guilt, the anger, the hate. You know, I've hated so long that I'm fearful that history might repeat itself. That I'll fail. The sins of the father . . ." Her voice trailed off. She nervously licked her dry lips, hesitantly raising her eyes to Nick's face, almost afraid to see the condemnation in his eyes. But there was no judgment to be found there; instead the gentleness in his voice reached out in soothing compassion.

"Yes, I can understand it all now." His strong hands cupped her tear-streaked face as he smiled into her anxious eyes.

Abby sighed. "That's why I get so upset when I get those computer dunning letters from Charge-X. Why I got so angry when you seemed to belittle my work. It makes the past seem so much closer and my responsibilities so much greater." She jerked her head from his grasp and averted her eyes. "I'm not even sure why I told you all this," she stammered self-consciously. "You know all my thoughts. It's almost as if you've broken into my mind."

"I won't abuse your trust, Abby," Nick told her, his voice deep with sincerity as he tenderly brushed the damp curls from her forehead. Then, as if to reinforce his promise, he put his lips against hers.

Abby shut her eyes and clung to him, needing him so much it was frightening. She seemed to have discovered a sense of security in his strong arms.

"It's time you shed this self-imposed guilt," he

71

murmured timeless seconds later as he cradled her body in his arms. "There was no way you had any control over what happened. You've got to put the past away and move forward."

Later that evening, Abby viewed the pink-and-pearl sunset with clear, untroubled eyes. Her apparent quietness at dinner had gone unnoticed by both her mother and her sister, who were animatedly telling her the details of a very successful day at the shop and how much they enjoyed John Maxwell's company.

Abby stretched joyfully, filling her lungs with the tangy salt air. For the first time she felt free. Free from the old hang-ups, the guilt, and the self-doubt. It was a rebirth. An awakening. She suddenly felt like laughing. She felt stronger, more stable and more self-confident than at any other time in her life.

Was it from just facing the past? Would she eventually have confided in someone, or was it this particular man?

Abby was convinced fate had finally smiled on her and sent Nick Maxwell. His quiet understanding, his allowance for less than perfection and yet not judging her in any way. They were able to empathize with each other; she trusted him completely. Was it possible their friendship had caught fire?

"I've been worried about you." Nick's voice broke into her thoughts. Startled, she turned and found him standing close behind her.

"I'm fine."

"I didn't want to leave you alone this afternoon."

"I needed time to pull myself together before Mom and Dee got home," she explained, knowing he'd understand. "They were quite charmed by your father," Abby added on a lighter note.

Nick chuckled. "Dad always had a way with the ladies."

"How about his son?" she asked hesitantly, turning her face back toward the sea.

"I've had my share too," came his slow response, "but only on a surface level." He paused, his voice deepening. "I never expected to become involved with anyone, really commit myself to anyone until a few days ago."

"Me?" Her breath caught in her throat.

"I found myself overly conscious of you right from the start. Does that sound crazy?" he asked. His hands slid to either side of her waist, turning her closer to his body.

"No," Abby whispered. "I was just thinking the same thing myself."

"I'm so very glad," he murmured, drawing her even closer to his muscular chest. His brown eyes never left her luminous gray ones until his dark head lowered and his mouth claimed hers with a stamp of possession that only reinforced the powerful physical attraction they had for each other. Abby's lips parted willingly, letting his tongue explore and taste the sweetness of her own hungry desire. Her hands slid up the taut muscles of his upper arm before tangling into the vibrant dark hair at the nape of his neck.

His lips moved slowly from her mouth across her soft, rounded cheek to the sensitive cord at the side of her ear. His tongue lightly, teasingly traced the small moon-shaped pierced earring it found there. His nose inhaled the heady fragrance of jasmine cologne as he buried his face in her soft curls.

She shivered slightly when his hands pulled her red cotton shirt free from the waistband of her shorts, sliding under to caress her smooth back before cupping her full, lace-covered breasts possessively. His mouth again took her lips with a hungry urgency of surrender. She moaned softly, responding willingly and naturally to his intimate caresses as the rising heat of dormant desire shuddered through her body.

After a few minutes Nick seemed to gain control of himself and pulled back. His breathing was ragged and she could feel the pounding of his heart as he held her head against his chest.

"I don't want to rush you into anything. I don't want you to be sorry." His voice was thick with controlled emotion.

Abby studied his face in the gray twilight and kissed him lightly on the corner of his mouth. She knew she'd never be sorry if Nick made love to her. He was already a part of her heart and soul. Loving him would make up for all the missing things in her life.

He smiled. "Come on. I'll walk you home."

CHAPTER SIX

There was a soothing rhythm to Nick's typing, even if it was liberally punctuated with errors. Abby smiled happily to herself before capping the tiny bottle of correction fluid she had been using. After four days of working with him her ears readily distinguished between his satisfied grunts of pleasure and his low-muttered frustrations.

The grunts seemed to be winning. Her eyes lowered to the top of the dining room table where the rapidly growing pile of completed manuscript pages lay. Nick's latest novel was an exceptional piece of work. The cleverly designed plot was masterly in its action, subplots, and unusual twists. His characters were not cardboard puppets but emotionally well-constructed individuals that vividly enhanced each page. His future readers would not be disappointed at his latest achievement.

They had been leaning against the veranda railing watching the sunset, a relaxing cup of after-dinner coffee in hand, when Nick first asked for her criticism. "Come on, Abby," he cajoled, his voice low and persuasive, "let me hear all your tough, cut-to-the-bone comments."

"What, and get a typewriter shoved down my throat?" she returned banteringly. "No, thanks. This is one time I'll just remain a silent reader."

"I'm asking for your opinion, Abby. I really want to know what that marvelous little brain of yours is really thinking."

Abby laughed. "Nick, you are impossible." She took a sip of her coffee and looked up to find his eyes focused with hypnotic penetration on her face. "So, you are just going to stare at me until I tell you, right?"

He flashed her a wide, wicked grin. Abby gave a resigned sigh. "Since I'm up to correcting chapter four, I can honestly say it is really magnificent." She took a deep breath. "I do think that the end of chapter one could be tighter. It doesn't seem to be up to the same standards as the rest of your work." She mentioned a few passages that had stuck in her mind.

Nick listened attentively, his eyes still focusing on her face, his mind carefully weighing each of her suggestions. For a long time he didn't say anything.

"Oh, Nick," Abby groaned, afraid she had insulted him terribly, "I told you I wanted to be just a reader."

He smiled at her, leaned over, and brushed his lips lightly across her forehead before returning to his typewriter. An hour later she had a revised first chapter to correct and a delicious sense of warmth growing inside of her at being a part of his creation.

To think that when she had met Nick Maxwell just a week ago she had thought him an enemy. Abby's shining gray eyes traveled from her bandaged left wrist to the diligently working man on the other side of the room, visually caressing the muscles on his back and shoulders through his close-fitting yellow terry pullover. She blessed that unfortunate accident with countless prayers. She had made a big emotional commitment. She had put her trust in someone; she had reached out and confided in Nick, both verbally and physically. She was able to show her feelings, open up to him with a closeness that made her feel nearer to him than she had ever been to anyone. Theirs was a strong friendship based on understanding and mutual confidence, sharing and forgiving. A companionship that also encompassed the powerful physical attraction they had for each other.

It was a dynamic process that transformed her from a cold, impersonal shell into a warm, loving, sensually awakened woman. Her discontent with herself had disappeared. Every time she saw Nick, Abby began to anticipate how good she was going to feel. She had thrown herself into their relationship wholeheartedly, transmitting all the energies she had used to guard herself, hide herself, and protect herself into enhancing their union. All thoughts of self-preservation and protection had vanished. She had found someone to complete her in the deepest possible sense.

Abby knew without a doubt that she loved Nick Maxwell. She shivered as her mind made that momentous declaration. She was positive he felt the same way.

It was there, in the way he openly discussed his fears and personal disappointments. They would walk on the beach at night and he would tell her about his first reporting assignment. It had been in the Far East, eighteen months spent with the misery and sadness of a wartorn people and land. He had been relieved when he was reassigned to the Mediterranean.

He had spent six months in France and Italy before taking another assignment in Greece. He had fallen in love with the Greek islands, especially Rhodes. He had lived a simple life with the villagers and worked with the fishermen. They had considered him one of their family. Together they shared the joys of weddings and births and the sorrow and pain of death.

He told her how these people had inspired him to write his first novel. Many of the book's characters were friends he had lived with, laughed with, and cried with. Abby never tired of listening to Nick. His vitality and eye for detail brought far-off lands and people alive with startling clarity. She felt privileged to gain an insight into his past, and it made their present a more equal relationship. Nick knew all about her former life and Abby knew everything about him. It was as if they were laying the foundation for a future together.

But they had their share of arguments too, Abby

grinned wryly. They were on opposite sides of the political fence; they argued over federal issues, state issues, economic issues, not budging in their views but always respecting each other's ideas.

They ended their days together with laughter, tender looks, and gentle caresses. Nick seemed to be taking his time with the physical side of their relationship, tempering their growing sensuality with a conscious regard for Abby's vulnerability.

Wednesday, her first day back at work, Abby had been delighted when Nick arrived to share her lunch hour. He had packed the rattan picnic hamper with fresh shrimp salad, warm rolls from the bakery, grapes, and iced tea. Abby had taken him up the twisting wrought iron staircase to the third floor turret room that housed a small collection of old books and journals that her aunt had acquired.

Nick had become particularly fascinated with a set of ten journals that belonged to a sea captain living in Camden during the early eighteenth century. His detailed account of colonial life and his sea voyages undertaken to carry his precious cargoes of tobacco back to England provided Nick with a fascinating journey back into time.

They had continued the habit of returning to their quiet haven each midday, Abby leaving behind the growing summer crowd of customers and the ringing telephone; Nick gratefully enjoying a respite from his typing and a chance to recharge his mind.

"Rapunzel would have unwound her golden hair for me to climb," he had teased earlier that day as they made their way up the circular staircase.

Abby turned and laughed, wrinkling her nose at him. "If you had wanted a girl with long tresses, you should have arrived a couple of weeks sooner," she retorted with mock annoyance, ruffling her short, sunkissed crop of brown curls.

The air-conditioned room with its amber-tinted windows cast a cool, golden glow of welcome on the couple. Nick once again had settled himself on a thick, plaid floor pillow and resumed his laborious readings of the journals that told of the Tidewater area over two centuries ago. Abby opted to wedge herself on the padded seat of the curved bay window and tried to choose what style of calendar she should order from an assortment of pre-season brochures that had arrived at the shop.

"Well," she gave a resigned sigh, one of seemingly a hundred she had emitted during the last hour. "I've finally decided to order recipes, ocean scenes, and cartoons with witty sayings," she announced, letting her spoon clank against the sides of the empty plastic yogurt container that she set on the floor. "That would just about cover women, men, and anything in between. What do you think, Nick?" She held up the three sample calendars she had selected for his opinion and was disconcerted by the odd expression on his rugged features.

"Oh, dear," she mused, her forehead puckering as she sifted through the folder on her lap, "do you think animals, antiques, and household hints would be better?" she asked, holding up three other choices.

Nick shook his head, his lips twisting into a lopsided smile.

"Don't you like any of them? Nick? Nick, why are you looking at me like that?" She stopped, watching in mesmerized fascination his catlike fluidity of movement as he joined her on the window seat.

The devilish glint in his brown eyes made her feel quite breathless. Her heart beat a frenzied tattoo as his fingers teasingly traced the sensitive blue vein on the inside of her bare arm before settling on the collar of her pink cotton blouse. "I just never thought watching anyone eat could be such an erotic experience."

"Nick." Abby's eyes widened perceptively, her cheeks suffusing with color under his disturbing, sensuous gaze and his outrageous statement. She heard rather than saw the brochures flutter to the floor, unable to concentrate on anything but the nearness of his face and the intoxicating aroma of his spicy aftershave.

His tongue lightly traced the outline of her trembling half-parted lips, tasting their sweetness before his mouth possessed hers in a long, sensuous kiss that made her feel dizzy and weightless. Her hands slid caressingly up his arms to his shoulders before linking around his neck, drawing him infinitely closer. "I'll have to make sure strawberry yogurt is put on the aphrodisiac list," she teased breathlessly before his mouth moved roughly back to claim hers with hungry urgency.

Flames of passion seared into her body wherever his skilled hands touched her, arousing her to equal his own savage desire. His hands moved slowly across her back, pulling her soft, pliant body closer to his own. He leaned back, taking her weight against his chest, until they were both reclining.

His mouth left hers to explore the soft curve of her jaw. She arched her throat, silently encouraging him to explore it with his lips. His teeth lightly nipped the swelling flesh of her rounded breasts revealed by the low neckline of her blouse, his tongue exploring the scented valley he found there. Her hands tangled in the vibrant depths of his dark hair, reveling in its thick, springy vitality. His mouth again sought hers, their breath becoming one in a unique dialogue. Her own passion was as heightened as his; only the thin material of their clothing separated them from complete fulfillment. Her body arched sensuously and pressed closer against him, unconsciously pleading for complete possession.

"Necking in the turret room?" Dee's amused voice sliced through the emotionally charged atmosphere like a cold shower. "Here I am starving to death, ready to faint, customers coming out of my ears, the phone hasn't stopped ringing . . . which reminds me, Nick, your father called. He wants you to stop at the market and pick up some groceries. I've got the list, he's making something French for dinner and—"

"One of these days I am going to get you totally and completely alone," Nick growled, his voice low and strained in her ear.

Released from his captive embrace, Abby gave her sister a rather pained smile, stood up, and straightened her bright floral wrap skirt. With supreme effort, she and Nick dutifully listened to Dee's tirade.

* * *

A plaintive wail from across the room brought Abby abruptly out of her pleasant reverie and back to reality and to the other occupants of Gull cottage. It was quite true, she admitted ruefully, they were never alone. Dee seemed to appear at the most inopportune times at the bookshop and with uncanny regularity on the beach when she and Nick took their evening stroll. Then there was her mother and his father.

John, who dabbled as a gourmet, insisted on sharing cooking or barbecuing chores with her mother, since the two families dined together every evening. When Abby came home from work, she'd find Claire and John disagreeing over the preparation of some recipe, how much seasoning should be used, or how long it should be cooked. During the evening they would continue their quarreling over a game of gin rummy or canasta or, as in tonight's case, a supposedly companionable game of Scrabble that had all the earmarks of a third world war!

Abby had to smile. Despite the increasing loudness of their voices, the constant on-going verbal battle had made her mother more outgoing, giving Claire a psychological and physical glow that was evident in her shining hazel eyes. It was true, the pattern and shape of their lives had changed since the Maxwell men had arrived.

"John, here it is, number eight," Claire repeated firmly, reading aloud from the rules printed in the top of the game box. "Any words found in a standard dictionary are permitted except those designated as foreign. And that little thirty-six point creation of yours is definitely foreign," she stated firmly.

"I don't know," he persisted. "It is a phrase that is used quite a lot."

"Where?" she snorted. "In ancient Rome?"

"All right, all right," he laughed easily, an unrepentant twinkle in his dark eyes as he took five tiles off the board. "I'll attempt to think of another word that will give me the same amount of generous points, while you reheat my coffee."

Claire gave him a mock glare, picked up the china mug, and headed for the kitchen. "Abby," she called, noting the kitchen clock. "It's just about time for Dan to come and pick you up. Did you tell him you'd be over here?"

"Yes, I did, Mom," she called, noting with feminine satisfaction that Nick's typing had abruptly stopped.

"Who is Dan?" Nick asked rather sharply, his eyes narrowing appreciatively as they took Abby in. For the first time he noticed the absence of her usual casual outfit of T-shirt and shorts. In their place was a slim-fitting black sundress with a side band of tricolored piping that followed the contours of her curving figure.

Abby gave him an innocent smile, reached for her purse, and extracted a large mirrored compact and a tube of russet lip gloss. "Dan Simmons is our high school football coach," she told him in a sweet voice, watching as the face in her mirror changed from one of calm contentment to mischievous delight.

He cleared his throat roughly at her statement,

thrusting his hands into the pocket of his tan jeans. "And you have a date with him tonight?"

"Did I say I had a date with him tonight?" she countered, her eyes opened innocently, her mouth quite prim and her ego flattered by his reaction.

"Why is he coming here?"

"Well," she drawled slowly, replacing her compact in her purse and viewing him circumspectly from under long, dark lashes, "Dan is also the head of the English department. Tonight, we are joining a few other teachers to go over this year's curriculum to see what books I should order. School starts in five weeks, Nick, and it's most annoying to have a horde of whining kids come into the bookshop saying they need a particular book for tomorrow that takes six weeks to get from the publisher."

Nick ran a self-conscious hand around his neck and tried to sound casual. "What does this guy look like? Have you known him long?"

"Dan?" Abby deliberately paused, lengthening the silence. "I've known him for quite some time. He's about your age. Very attractive, more the blond beach-boy type . . ." She heard his annoyed grunt and tried hard to stifle the laughter that was threatening to take control of her voice. "He also has the most adorable wife and a set of eight-year-old twin boys who buy out my superhero comic book section each month."

"Why you little stinker," he charged exasperatedly, his hand snaking out to capture her arm. Nick's eyes crinkled attractively at the corners and Abby could see the twitching of his lips that allayed any

85

anger over her flirtatious teasing. Any further retaliation he had in mind was interrupted by the door bell.

Dan Simmons, much to Nick's chagrin, did indeed match Abby's description. Despite the complete innocence of the situation, Nick couldn't seem to help himself and asked "How's the wife and kids?" as he shook hands during their introduction.

Abby failed to swallow her light bubble of laughter and hastily pulled a much confused English teacher toward the door before turning and blowing Nick a saucy fairwell kiss.

Abby gave a final wave as Dan's car backed down her gravel driveway and sped off into the night. It had been a very successful evening, she thought happily. The teachers had been most cooperative about supplying her with their prospective reading assignments. They were anxious to get opening plans under way so they could enjoy the few weeks left of their summer vacation. Abby had come away with an order that was destined to turn into lucrative sales during the coming fall and winter months.

"I see you've finally decided to come home," growled a deep masculine voice from out of the darkness. She jumped nervously, then laughed with relief as Nick's rangy figure loomed out of the shadows on her front porch.

"It turned out to be a very productive and profitable night," she grinned at him, patting her straw bag smugly.

His sinewy arm slid around her waist, guiding her

up the stairs toward a far corner of the porch. He pushed her against the wooden railing. "And you didn't mind prefacing the evening with a little teasing at my expense," Nick reflected silkily. He plucked the purse out of her fingers and dropped it on the painted wood floor. His body crushed against hers, effectively forming a barrier against any escape.

"Who, *moi?*" Abby batted her lashes innocently, her hand in an affected pose against her breast as she looked up into his strong features, visible in the silvery moonlight.

The low deep timbre of his laughter brought alive that warm delicious curling sensation. Unconsciously, she arched her body invitingly toward his.

His teeth flashed in a wolfish smile, strong and white against the tan of his skin. "You have to take your punishment," he threatened huskily, his eyes glittering dangerously as they roamed over her luminous features. He bent his head, his lips slowly and torturously moving along her jaw line from the tiny gold ball in her ear to finally capture her softly parted lips.

Abby found herself responding quite naturally and uninhibitedly; her hands locked together at the small of his back, pressing her seemingly boneless body intimately against his muscular length. His thighs were taut beneath the thin material of his trousers.

Their lips and tongues explored, allowing passion and desire to grow in exquisite ecstasy. Nick's hands slid around Abby's waist, lightly stroking the rounded curves of her buttocks through the clingy material of her dress, pressing her into more intimate contact than she had ever experienced, making her in no doubt of the extent of his passion and the power she had over him.

"I was jealous as hell tonight." His voice was low and ragged, his lips nuzzling the sensitive skin under her ear.

Abby's fingers slid around his wide leather belt, clutching it for support. She rubbed her soft cheek against his beard-roughened jaw, hoping to calm both Nick and the aroused sensations coursing through her body.

"I was just teasing," she whispered, her teeth playfully nipping his earlobe.

"I know," he muttered, his fingers gently brushing aside the wide straps of her dress so his mouth could sample the sweet softness of her skin. "But just the thought of another man going out with you, touching you . . . well, it made me feel very primitive." He grimaced wryly.

Her finger silenced his lips, her eyes mirroring the depth of her feelings for him. "You must know you are the only man in my life. There is no one else. . . ."

"But there could be," he interrupted roughly. "You've no idea the lustful looks you get from the male customers who come into your shop and on the beach—"

She gave a low, throaty laugh. Her hand slid slowly, teasingly over his chest before locking with its mate behind his strong neck. "The only lustful reaction I want is from you," she teased, her lips pressing his eyelids closed before moving down to claim his mouth in a deep kiss that again set fire to her blood and sent a tremor shuddering through her body in answer to the one she felt in his.

An obscene flooding of light and the creaking of the warped wooden front door had them instantly, almost guiltily, jumping apart.

"I was just telling Claire I thought I heard someone on the front porch," John's voice floated out to the two heavily breathing figures.

Nick coughed, cleared his throat, and with great difficulty managed a reasonably civil smile and tone. "I was just telling Abby that she has to get her stitches removed tomorrow. I thought I'd take her to the clinic myself. We all know what a procrastinator she is when it comes to medical attention."

Abby bent over to reclaim her fallen straw bag and favored Nick with a sweet smile. "What time did you say you were coming to the shop?"

"About one," he replied, the corners of his shapely mouth twitching with suppressed humor.

"Hey," Dee's voice caroled from inside, "the oven timer's buzzing."

"Okay," John returned, motioning Nick and Abby to come into the living room. "Now you'll see just how a proper English scone should taste."

"My own always seemed quite sufficient," Claire retaliated with spirit.

"But then you've never tasted my recipe," he told her, heading for the kitchen. "I got this from the chef on the *Queen Elizabeth*."

"You used the same ingredients, John. I honestly don't see how it could taste any different," Claire retorted, following his broad frame. "How did you do at the meeting tonight, Abby?" she called, looking back over her shoulder at her daughter.

"Fine, Mom, just fine," Abby answered dutifully. "It looks like a full house," she muttered to Nick.

He slid a comforting arm around her shoulders. They gave a shared sigh of futile resignation before slowly following their bickering parents into the kitchen.

CHAPTER SEVEN

"Abigail Faith Wetherby." Hearing her full name spoken in such a condemning tone from the thin lips of Leona DeWitt caused Abby to roll her gray eyes in anticipated agony. "Do you realize that you are contributing to the moral corruption of this community by having this . . . this material on display!" The short, barrel-built woman continued in a droning, nasal tone that grated on Abby's ears.

She took a deep breath, exhaled slowly while she counted her pink-tipped toes that were visible on her white-sandal-clad feet. Abby put down the inventory sheet and walked over to the book bins. "What seems to be the problem?" she asked, giving Mrs. DeWitt the friendliest smile she could manage.

"This . . . this trash. I found it in the family reference section. How you have the nerve to even order such a book." She shuddered disgustedly, dropping the offending matter into Abby's outstretched palm. "Does your mother know you have such obscene material on display?"

The obscene material, Abby noted wryly, was a plastic-wrapped copy of a sex manual that was currently on the best seller list. "It is written by two very prominent and accredited physicians, Mrs. DeWitt," Abby told the irate woman. "As you can see, it is on the topmost shelf, not at eye level, and very sturdily sealed," she continued calmly, trying to ignore the impatient tapping of the elder woman's black orthopedic shoe. "Anyone under eighteen is not allowed to examine the display copy we have under the register. We are very careful—"

"Really?" Mrs. DeWitt sucked in a sharp breath, her aquiline nose pinched downward, almost hooking her upper lip. Her shoulders went rigid under her plain white, high-collared longsleeved blouse and her chubby fingers removed an infinitesimal speck of lint that was offending her pristine navy blue skirt. "This isn't the only disgusting book I've located. There are at least six others in your *family* section that are offensive. Heaven only knows what else is lurking about in this store ready to corrupt Camden's youth." One pale blue, gimlet eye looked with askance at Abby's sleeveless, scooped-neck, white knit shirt and daisy-flowered slim-fitting slacks. "You do rather resemble your Bohemian Aunt Emily, don't you?"

Abby mentally congratulated herself for keeping her temper under control. It was patently useless to argue with the woman, so Abby pasted a tight-lipped smile on her face and pretended to listen to Mrs. DeWitt's filibuster, while her brain kept chanting the retailer's motto: the customer is always right.

Abby's eyes glinted mischievously. She suddenly slammed the large paperback on the counter, the explosive sound instantly silencing the woman. "You know, you're quite right," she announced. "Just as soon as I get through with this book inventory, I'll go over this entire section. In fact, I'll let my mother do it," she said matter-of-factly.

Mrs. DeWitt's head bobbed in agreement. "Claire is extremely sensible," she stated, unnecessarily raising a hand to check on any gray strands escaping from her tightly rolled and pinned hairstyle.

"Yes, Mother is extremely sensible," Abby echoed and gently eased the satisfied woman toward the shop's front door. "I'm sure she'll take your comments and put them to good use." She smiled sweetly, biting her tongue to keep from telling the woman exactly where she'd like to put her suggestions. She gave Mrs. DeWitt a bright little wave before slamming the glass door shut.

"Aren't you the same girl who gave me a lecture on book banning and censorship the other day?" a masculine voice intoned dryly from the rear alcove.

Abby instantly smiled at the sight of Nick's rangy figure, casually clad in white tennis shorts and a navy T-shirt, leaning indolently against the back wall. "You've got to start wearing noisier shoes," she teased, her gray eyes shining with unconcealed pleasure.

"What was that all about?" he queried interestedly, joining Abby at the counter.

"That was Mrs. Leona DeWitt, Camden's chronic complainer." She wrinkled her nose at him. "She comes in once every full moon to criticize the shop. Last month, she lit into me over the cookbook section."

"Now what the devil could she possibly find offensive about cookbooks?" Nick frowned thoughtfully.

"We had too many featuring wines and spirits and didn't I know I was contributing to the moral decadence of Camden," Abby dutifully recited with a straight face. She shrugged her shoulders and sighed. "It's easier to agree with her. I just tell her what she wants to hear and that placates her for another month. You have no idea how many Mrs. DeWitts there are in the world until you have to deal with the wide variety of personalities that come into this shop."

A shadow crossed Nick's face. He remembered playing the same game with Bill York in the computer department. He bit his lip. He still had that problem to resolve with Abby, and the longer he waited the harder it was going to be to tell her who he really was.

Abby retrieved the oversized paperback from the counter. "Say, who unchained you from your typewriter?" she teasingly scolded, walking back toward the family reference bin.

"I'm finished," Nick announced with a grin. "The book's all boxed and set to go to my editor," he added, strolling over to the magazine rack and selecting the latest issue of *Business Week.*

"Wait a minute. Don't I get to see the final chapter," she wailed, feeling hurt by his sudden secrecy.

"I never give away my surprise endings," he teased. "I'm bringing it to New York tomorrow," came his offhanded comment, while his eyes read the magazine's table of contents.

Abby swallowed hard, nervously running her tongue over suddenly dry lips. "You mean *mailing* it to New York," she corrected him hopefully.

"Hmm?" Nick kept reading the stock market summary. "No. I was lucky enough to get an early morning flight."

Despite the profusion of fluorescent lighting, the bookshop suddenly grew very dark. Abby continued with her outward motions of straightening a shelf, struggling to make her voice sound natural against the deathly silence of her heart. "Yes, yes, that was very fortunate." Her words sounded brittle and hollow. She swallowed the growing lump in her throat. "You certainly got that book done in record time."

"Not really," came his abstract remark. "I had it eighty percent done before I came here and your help just made the work go that much faster."

She tightly closed her eyes, willing time to stand still, to keep Nick here, close to her until she became as important to him as he had become to her. "Your little holiday comes to a sudden close. You've accomplished quite a lot in three weeks." Her voice fought for composure, but her trembling lips betrayed her lacerated emotions.

"Hmm. I did manage to get a lot done," Nick idly agreed, turning the glossy page to finish an interesting article on treasury notes.

Abby felt herself sway and hastily focused her misting eyes on the cover of the book she was holding. Her nerveless fingers delicately traced the cover's pencil drawing of entwined lovers.

He had accomplished a lot. In three weeks Nick had become her friend, her confidant; now, she would never know him as her lover. They had shared all the little things, and for the first time in her life she had felt the all-consuming desire to become closer to a man, to become part of his life physically. She heard Nick's voice as if from the end of a tunnel. "What . . . what did you say?" Her own was a low whisper, barely squeezing through the constricted muscles of her throat.

"I said I'd though we'd celebrate. Go out for dinner tonight," he repeated, completely oblivious to the emotional upheaval going on across the room. "I heard about a fantastic Greek restaurant about ten miles up the coast. I might even tell you the plot twist in my final chapter," came his teasing rejoinder.

"Final chapter"—that distressing refrain echoed over and over, hanging in the air like invisible bricks, building a wall that would ultimately divide the two of them forever. Tonight would be her final chapter, the final memory to a time which would be the most important in her life.

Abby wondered what would happen if she threw herself into his arms and begged him to stay. She shook her head roughly, clearing away that ridiculous notion. Wasn't she always proclaiming her independence and her assertiveness? Why, she was no adolescent in the throes of puppy love. She was nearly a quarter of a century old; old enough to accept the reality of the situation and its grief.

Maybe Nick was the kind of man who couldn't stay with just one woman. He had said in the beginning he wasn't looking for a summer love affair. Well, neither was she. She wasn't just in love with him for the month of July; she wanted him for the eleven other months as well. For a lifetime. If she said anything that would make him feel obligated to stay, he might get bored and restless, then resentful. She'd hate that. She didn't want to be responsible for killing his spirit, for changing him from the man she'd fallen in love with.

Abby fought back the deadly feeling of depression that had been her nemesis for so long. Her feelings for Nick were so strong that falling out of love was going to require intense concentration. In loving him she had lost herself. She would have to adjust. It would take a lifetime to forget him, to stop dreaming about him. She'd have to do something. She'd volunteer at the library, she'd redecorate the house, rearrange the bookshop. She'd force herself to recharge and rethink. Didn't the experts say there was no such thing as just one person in your life?

But somehow, she knew. Somehow she was positive that Nick Maxwell was the only man she would ever love. She would have to deal with the emptiness and the loneliness.

As for tonight? Just the thought of a farewell dinner made her feel nauseated, but she'd choke one down. Just for tonight she would let her dream continue. She would laugh and smile; she would be witty and clever; she would be the best dinner companion he ever had. She would flirt outrageously and say something sophisticated in a carefully practiced blasé voice like: "Now, I won't have to worry about getting a hotel room when I visit New York. I can always stay with you."

Nick would laugh, his eyes would crinkle attractively, and he would say, "Come any time. My house is your house."

She would say: "How about a week from Tuesday, with just my toothbrush." And she would go. She promised herself she would get the first plane available and go to New York.

But for tonight she would let her dream continue and when tomorrow came and Nick left, well, she would handle that too. She would be all right, eventually.

He glanced up from his magazine, his mouth twisting into a frown over Abby's lack of an answer. "Listen, if you've got another restaurant you would rather go to for dinner, just say the word," Nick said, his eyes on her rigid back. "We can always try this Greek place when I come back."

"You . . . you're coming back?"

Two familiar arms wrapped themselves around her waist, hugging her in the most reassuring manner she could ever imagine. "Yes, I'll be back. I'm only going to be gone five days, a week at the most. What did you think? That I was leaving for good? That this was the end of us?" She felt his arms tighten, instinctively sensing her doubt.

A dark cloud had been lifted, sunlight streamed into the room as Abby's heart began pumping life back into her body. She was able to breathe again. A reprieve—but for how long? She firmly pushed that thought from her mind, refusing to think about it. She lay against him, hearing the steady beat of his heart against her shoulder, her fingers threading through the curling mat of dark hair on his arms. "Yes," she acknowledged at length, "I thought you were leaving."

She was turned around. Nick's dark eyes staring into her own smoky orbs for an interminable length of time. His voice was unusually gentle. "I want to get the book and some other business settled. It will take a few days, that's all." He smiled. "So how about it? Dinner at the Aegis?"

She laughed and nodded. "You will have to do me one little favor."

He raised a quizzical dark brow.

"Here, take this." She shoved the book into his hand.

"You want me to read this for tonight?" he asked dryly, looking pointedly at the sex manual.

Abby gave a low chuckle. "No. You could probably add a few chapters though." She grinned, blushing at her own suggestive teasing. "I want you to watch the store for a few minutes until your father brings my mother back."

"Okay," he nodded, mystified by her request, "but where are you going?"

"The Aegis is a very fancy place, Mr. Maxwell, and," Abby drawled, gliding away from his side and quickly getting her purse from under the counter, "I haven't a thing to wear!" She gave him a cheery little wave before slipping out the door.

CHAPTER EIGHT

"I should have called and made reservations," Nick ruefully admitted to Abby, watching the slow queue of couples ahead of them give their names to the maître d' before retiring to the lounge for what clearly looked like a long wait. "It seems my idea of a romantic dinner for two was not very original."

She gave a low laugh, linking her arm in his. "Well, our commerce department has been telling people for years that Virginia is for lovers. This just proves their point."

"This is a restaurant—not a motel," he returned dryly.

"It's all in the atmosphere." She breathed dreamily, her hand sweeping toward the two scantily draped marble statues of Greek goddesses that adorned the lobby's subtly lit waterfall, lush potted ferns, and fig trees that gave the room a gardenlike appearance with the elegant quarry stone tile under-foot. "Of course, the Aegis is famous for their food and I'm certainly hungry for . . . food," she added teasingly.

"Is that a fact, Miss Wetherby," he drawled in a dangerously silky voice that instantly sent a quiver through her veins. "I think I can manage to give you a little romance for your dessert."

"I was thinking more of baklava," Abby smiled innocently at him.

"Wait until you see me by candlelight," he grinned wolfishly, his brown eyes dancing with undisguised humor.

"I'm sure you'll prove irresistible," she told him, her fingers automatically tightening on his arm. He certainly looked irresistible, Abby thought shame-lessly. His raw masculinity was heightened by an impeccably tailored double-breasted oyster-toned suit, a pale blue shirt, and a harmoniously striped silk tie.

"I think we are going to have a long wait in the lounge," Nick muttered as they neared the maître d's discretely lit lectern.

"Why don't you just tell him who you are."

His heart stopped. He inhaled a swift breath. "Who I am?" Nick asked her, slowly, carefully.

"Hmm. I'm sure they wouldn't let a famous au-thor wait."

He cleared his throat, his fingers easing the knot of his tie that had grown unbearably tight. "I don't think it would work here, Abby." *No, not here,* Nick thought. In New York either of his names would have meant instant seating even in the most exclusive restaurant.

"I still think you should try," Abby continued blithely. "Ask, no, demand one of the window tables. The view of the sea is just breathtaking. They have outdoor colored spotlights that highlight the breakers."

His forehead puckered and he eyed her suspiciously. "Have you been here before?"

She merely opened her eyes in wondered innocence and nudged him toward the maitre d'.

"Good evening, sir, your name?" The short, balding man in a white evening jacket looked up from his heavily inked ledger at his next customer. His brown eyes moved past the tall man to focus on the dancing gray eyes of his curly haired companion.

The lady favored him with an outrageous wink. "We'd love a window seat," Abby told him, giving him her most dazzling smile, which was eagerly returned.

"But of course, right this way," came his richly accented reply. He picked up two menus, leaving a perplexed Nick to follow his stocky figure into the main dining room.

The massive room was designed to resemble a glittering palazzo. Dimly lit crystal chandeliers shimmered like a sky of diamonds overhead, while the strategically arranged tables gave the patrons a breathtaking view of the ocean through a massive wall of curved windows.

"It's your dress," Nick growled in her ear as they slowly wound their way through the crowded room, their feet silenced by the plush gold and red carpeting.

"Don't be silly," she whispered in return. "Why, I just threw this little old thing on."

"You throw awfully well," came his dry rejoinder.

"I didn't think you even noticed my new dress."

She heard him grunt and felt a possessive hand spread against the base of her spine. "Oh, I noticed your dress. Even the waiters are noticing your dress. You're every man's idea of a diversion in that damn dress."

Abby smiled, feeling ridiculously lightheaded and very feminine. Despite being a hasty last-minute purchase, the dress seemed to have that couturier's stamp of design. The saleswoman had said it needed a tall, well-built figure to do it justice; and for once Abby was glad she wasn't flat and model-thin.

It was a simple little black dress, its sensuous material hugging her curving silhouette, a narrow silver belt highlighted her waist. The daringly cut V-shaped bodice was held by ridiculously thin silver straps. Provocative red toenails peeped out from her narrow-heeled black sandals.

Despite the slightly heavier evening makeup she had applied, Abby's face was soft and luminous. She had rimmed her gray eyes with kohl, then shadowed the lids with a shimmering dust of silver. Her lips glistened with an inviting glow of apricot gloss. The tiny rhinestone chips in her ears rivaled the brillance of diamonds and a shining aureole of curls framed her face.

Before they were even seated, Abby heard her

name called. Much to Nick's astonishment, he watched as his beautiful companion was encased in a bear hug by another white tuxedo-clad restaurant employee.

"Stavros," she squealed, "you're crushing the breath out of me."

"Ah, but you are too thin," came his deep voice. "You should come here to eat more often. We'll fatten you up tonight." He turned his silver head toward Nick, eyeing him with parental scrutiny. "Who's this?"

"Stavros Karamanlis, this is Nick Maxwell." Abby smiled.

"He is special?"

"Very."

"Well, then." Stavros waved aside Nick's outstretched hand, grabbed his shoulders, and pulled him into a strong embrace. "This one, she is like my own daughter," he informed Nick, giving him a hearty slap on the back. "This is the first summer she has not worked here. It makes us all sad. But tonight we celebrate the return of family."

Stavros picked up the menus from the table. "Dimitri, take these away. I will order for you both." He turned to Nick. "You do want my Greek food?" A thick silver brow arched speculatively.

"I haven't had any good Greek food since I left Rhodes."

"Dimitri, did you hear, he's been to our Rhodes!" Stavros's dark eyes grew warm and moist in the sharp planes and angles of his deeply tanned face. "This is Dimitri Androkitis, my brother-in-law," he told Nick, introducing the short maître d' who had just finished seating Abby. "Have you ever been to Lindhos?"

"Isn't that a small fishing village on the southern coast?" Nick asked. At Dimitri's and Stavros's dual nods, he added, "I stopped at a *kafenío*—a coffee shop—" he translated for Abby's benefit. "It's a lovely place."

Stavros clapped his large hands together, heedless of the interested stares of the other customers. "This is indeed a night to celebrate. Dimitri," he ordered, "bring the ouzo. I'll be right back."

"You could have told me this was the restaurant where you worked." Nick smiled wryly at Abby as he seated himself at their small gold-cloth-covered table.

"I thought men liked women to surprise them," she countered innocently.

His hand reached out to warmly capture hers. "You surprise me every day. Life with you would never be dull."

Abby studied his face in the flickering glow of the candlelit room. Was that declaration a promise of things to come? They were so emotionally involved. Abby was often surprised by the growing ache inside her for the need of physical involvement. She had always been afraid to express her own sexuality until she had fallen in love with Nick. Now it seemed the most natural thing in the world to not only share her thoughts with him, but her body as well.

Stavros's sudden return made her realize where she was. He had brought an extra place setting and turned a chair around from a nearby table and proceeded to join them. "I've told Dioni and Nikos that you are here," he grinned at Abby. "They will cook their hearts out for you." He turned to Nick. "Now you will taste the best of Greece. Moussaka, dolmáthes, and tirópita that will make you cry with their rich flavor. You like sea food?" At their affirmative response, he said, "You will taste the wonders of kténia and achivádes pilafi—that's scallops and clams over rice. Dioni makes a baklava so light it would reach the gods on Olympus. Then you will have strong, sweet coffee that was the only good to come from the Turks."

Course followed upon course, as did their laughter and stories. Nick told of his travels through Greece and Stavros added his own memories of his homeland. All of the waiters and the kitchen staff made trips to the table to see Abby and it was quite apparent they were the center of attention.

They were sitting in companionable silence over the foamy Turkish coffee and dessert wine of mavrodaphne when the languid strains of dance music assailed their ears.

"If you had come Wednesday night you would have heard real music, not this . . . this disco that the customers want," Stavros told them gruffly.

"That doesn't sound like disco to me. It sounds like very romantic dance music." Abby smiled across the table at Nick.

"Ah, but Wednesday was the Greek bouzouki. We even broke plates like in the old days. You would have—" Stavros stopped, realizing his two compan-

107

ions were staring at each other, seemingly in a world of their own. His eyes narrowed as he lit a thin cheroot, watching the smoke curl away. "Listen, why don't you two try out that music. I must check on the kitchen." He pushed back his chair, bent over, and kissed Abby before disappearing among the other diners.

Nick got up and drew Abby to her feet, their bodies moving in perfect rhythm to the slow, sensual beat of the music. "Do you realize this is the first time we've been totally alone since we got here?" he murmured into her ear.

She peeped at him through her long, darkened lashes. "We do seem to have the uncanny knack of attracting a crowd," she agreed ruefully.

His right hand moved from gently caressing the exposed skin at the nape of her neck to slide warmly across her bare shoulders before settling at the low curve of her back. She pressed herself tighter against him, feeling the response of his hardening muscle.

Her fingers delicately traced the line of his shirt collar. She nestled her face in the curve of his neck. The scent of his woodsy aftershave was a potent aphrodisiac to her already-heightened emotions.

She sighed contendedly, not wanting to think how long and lonely the next week would be without Nick. She wondered if he would miss her, feel her loss. Would absence make the heart grow fonder?

"Do you think Stavros and the rest of your friends would be insulted if we left and spent what little time the rest of the evening affords all to ourselves?"

Nick's voice was low and vibrant, his breath tickling her ear.

"The Greeks are a very passionate people," Abby told him, the black pupils of her eyes dominating the smoky irises. "Somehow, I think they would understand."

It was raining when they finally left the Aegis, a soft, slanting rain that subtly cooled the hot July night air. Hand in hand, laughing like children, they ran, skipping over the slowly forming puddles in the parking lot to the glistening Mercedes. Abby snuggled her damp shoulders against the plush, climate-controlled interior of the car. She felt content and enviably happy. Her eyes half-closed, her head leaning against Nick's shoulder, she listened to the increasing tempo of nature's showery serenade on their homeward drive.

After listening to five miles of her cajoling and badgering, Nick laughingly relented and slowly divulged the final chapter of his novel in a kind of verbal shorthand. Abby sat up, completely enthralled. The book's twist was totally unexpected and left her spellbound and gasping.

"You are incredibly clever," she told him breathlessly, her eyes glowing with admiration as she settled herself close to him.

"Yes, I know," he grinned. "Now, what the devil —" The amusement in his voice died and his mouth twisted into a frown when he turned the Mercedes into the driveway of Gull Cottage. "It looks like Dad is having a party."

Abby peered through the swishing windshield

wipers, immediately recognizing the small contingent of cars parked on the gravel drive. "It's my mother's bridge group," she told him, her forehead puckering in recollection. "I think Mom said something about having their final tournament at your place because Dee's having a slumber party at ours and—" Her voice trailed off weakly.

Nick turned to her in disbelief. "Do you mean to tell me both of the cottages are occupied tonight?"

She nodded slowly.

His hand slammed down hard on the upholstered seat, causing her to jump hastily to one side. "I don't believe this! I figured we could have a little time to ourselves somewhere along the line this evening."

"The bridge game usually ends a little after midnight," she told him consolingly.

"Wonderful!" came his sarcastic rejoinder. He looked at the digital clock. "It's almost that now. I've got to catch the seven o'clock flight and I need a little sleep." He looked out at the inclement weather with utter disgust on his rugged face. "We can't even go for a walk on the beach the way it's coming down now."

The persistent, angry drumming of Nick's long fingers against the wooden dashboard threatened to drown out the now heavily falling rain.

Abby sighed, her shoulders slumping dejectedly. This was definitely not the way to end an otherwise dream of an evening. Her disheartened gaze watched the wide rivulets of water course down the windshield. Gradually her discouraged expression changed to one of joyful anticipation.

She cleared her throat and straightened against the plush seat. "I always thought sitting in a car with the rain dancing on the roof, the moonlight wafting through the windows . . . well, that always seemed very romantic," she said to no one in particular.

The drumming fingers stopped. Nick turned his head and in a rather brusque voice said; "Abby, I am thirty-six years old. I refuse to end my evening necking in a car like a teen-ager!"

She hastily swallowed a bubble of laughter and with commendable aplomb managed a blasé tone. "You're right. I don't know whatever possessed me to even think of such a thing. I mean, thirty-six, why you've got one foot in the grave. You probably were never good at necking in cars anyway, and forgot whatever technique you had, so—" Her neck snapped sharply when Nick released a lever propelling the wide seat backward.

"Oh, really," he drawled dangerously, his deep voice acquiring that low, sensuous timbre that had such a calamitous effect on her nervous system. "That's a most provocative challenge, Miss Wetherby," he continued silkily, his eyes glittering in the dimly lit interior. "I hope you are up to it."

With hypnotic fascination, Abby watched Nick shed his white suit jacket and pull off his silk tie, tossing them both carelessly toward the rear seat. His eyes darkened, smoldering with naked desire. The sensuous boldness of his firmly molded mouth caused her to shiver against the burning fires that threatened to consume her own body.

His hands lightly slid up her bare arms, his fingers

111

deftly brushing aside her slender straps before releasing the constricting zipper at the back of her black dress. The soft folds of material drifted down to settle around her waist when she reached out to release the buttons on his silk shirt. Her hands parted the material so her fingers could thread through the dark mat of hair on his rugged chest.

Slowly they drew together, her head rolling to one side as his lips sought the rapidly beating pulse at the base of her throat. His mouth moved languidly over her neck, breathing in the haunting scent of her perfume before hungrily seeking the sweetness of her softly parted lips.

His rugged body gently guided her downward until they were both lying across the wide front seat, their legs as intimately intertwined as their arms.

Abby wriggled out of her sandals, letting her silk-stocking-clad foot teasingly slide up Nick's leg, her toes nuzzling against the taut muscles of his calf. Her breasts shuddered under his hard tongue and skilled fingers, while her own hands caressed the muscles of his bare chest. Her trembling fingers followed the trail of hair down his stomach to lightly outline his navel.

She moaned with unconcealed desire when his lips sought the sensitive, hardened nipples of her full breasts. Reveling in this dangerous physical delight, Abby willingly lost herself in the exquisite pleasure of Nick's masterly touch.

"Abby, you've turned into a wanton child," he muttered thickly, his lips nipping the sensitive skin at the base of her ear.

She giggled, half-closed her eyes, and moved her head, rubbing her cheek against the hair-roughened warmth of his naked chest. "I was wrong," she murmured. "You haven't lost your touch. We've fogged up all the windows." She sighed, feeling the sensuous contentment of Nick's hand as it gently stroked her back. Her own breathing was labored under the torrent of emotions Nick was able to arouse in her. She had never thought she possessed the primitive yearnings that ignited her body whenever he touched her. The thought of being without him for an entire week depressed her. "Do you really have to be gone so long?"

"I'm afraid so, honey," he conceded reluctantly. "I've got a lot of things to straighten out, including a few for my father. The three weeks of mail I've got to sift through should keep me very busy all by itself."

"Maybe during the day, but what about at night?" she asked lightly, her fingers moving to trace the planes and angles of his strong face. "I understand those city women are very fascinating."

"You're just about all the fascination I can handle these days," he grinned, his white teeth flashing devilishly in the semi-darkness. "What about you?"

"Me?" her voice echoed in surprise.

"Yes, you!" Nick retorted, turning so that his powerful torso took complete advantage over her soft, pliant form. "I told you I noticed all those lascivious male vacationers eyeing you at the bookshop."

She gave a low, throaty laugh, wiggling enticingly

beneath him. "I guess you'll just have to dust me for fingerprints when you come back," she teased, sliding her arms lovingly around his neck.

"I'd better find only my own," his voice growled warningly, his mouth branding its possessive ownership on her eagerly parted lips.

Sounds penetrated their ears, laughter and squeals against the rain, coupled with the slamming of car doors. They sat up. "It looks like their party's over," Nick muttered hoarsely, brushing back a dark lock of hair that had fallen across his forehead.

"Ours too," Abby intoned sadly. She readjusted her twisted dress and settled back into a more proper passenger position.

Nick turned the ignition key, snapping the powerful engine to life, reversing the Mercedes back down the drive and maneuvering it onto the wide gravel shoulder. His arm pulled her back against the warmth of his body while they waited for the bridge players to depart.

He took a deep breath and ran his left hand around the back of his neck. "Listen." His voice was urgent, his eyes staring straight out the windshield, his features carved with dogged determination. "I've got to tell you something. I've been meaning to tell you right from the beginning and I don't want to leave with this unsaid. I—"

Abby's fingers stilled his lips. "I don't need any reassurance about our relationship. I don't need any promises in the dark. Tell me when you come home." Her hand pulled his face around, the dashboard lights casting a golden glow on her smiling features,

114

love and desire mirrored in her luminous gray eyes. She reached up and pulled his neck down so her lips could once more seek the joyous contentment of his.

CHAPTER NINE

"Thank you," Abby gasped with undisguised relief when the bookshop door swung open from within. She struggled with a large, unwieldy carton that seemed determined to wedge itself in the doorway. Exhaling a long breath, she lowered the box to an empty floor area, letting her beige canvas espadrilled foot finish pushing her heavy burden to one side.

Abby wiped the back of her hands across her perspiring cheeks, letting her lungs deeply inhale the cool, refreshing air-conditioned atmosphere of the bookshop. Her nose twitched at the rather overpowering, albeit, expensive fragrance wafting from her benefactor. Her gray eyes located a petite stranger, elegantly clad in a sleeveless, nubby-textured pale pink summer suit and a wide-brimmed straw hat that only enhanced the daintiness of her pale blond features.

"It's about time you returned, Abby," Dee's voice caroled in an unnecessarily loud tone from behind the register.

"The department store was much busier than I had anticipated," she told her sister. A sudden stopping of movement caused Abby to turn her head. She found the strikingly attractive customer had paused in the open doorway, suddenly taking a renewed interest in her appearance. She gave the woman a rather forced, tentative smile, adjusted the mandarin collar on her multistriped blouse, and uncomfortably rubbed her hands along the sides of her pale lilac slacks.

The blonde arched a delicately plucked brow and slid on a pair of oversize sunglasses, her mouth twisting into a thin-lipped smile before she glided out the door.

"Wasn't she just fabulous?" Dee gushed with even more enthusiasm than usual. "I'm positive I saw that suit in *Vogue*. Did you see her shoes? I'm sure they were hand made, and that fabulous hat?"

"I can see she made quite an impression on you." Abby smiled indulgently at her sister.

"I'll say." Dee grinned. "She came in just a few minutes after you left. I watched her the whole time."

"Studied her, you mean," Abby said dryly, leaning over the counter to tuck her purse into an empty drawer.

"Whatever," her sister retorted. "Anyway, she wandered around, looked at all the displays, and shuffled through the new magazines."

117

"But did she buy anything?" Abby asked archly.

"She was interested in the rare books."

"They aren't for sale," Abby interrupted.

"Well, I know that," Dee returned huffily, "but no one else has to. I just told her that we had a rare, fabulous collection that were under lock and key and only you could show them, only with an appointment, of course."

"Dee! You're outrageous." Abby laughed. "Fabulous collection, indeed. The gold decal lettering on the windows are probably worth more than our rare books. They're just journals written by local sailors and farmers. Their only value is historical. You know I'm going to give them to the new library when it's completed."

"Oh, pooh!" Dee grinned impishly. "Listen, she really believed me. I was treated with more importance from then on, I'll tell you."

"Oh?"

"I bet I could have sold her one of our paintings, if they weren't all sold already. Anyway, she asked about the artists, said we had a fabulous store and thought business must be very good with all the vacationers. You know," Dee mused thoughtfully, "the more I think about it—the way she kept asking me questions. I bet she's a reporter or . . . or a gossip columnist," she announced brightly, wriggling back on the wooden counter stool.

"Why, because she was wearing a hat?" Abby queried with amusement, her fingers automatically straightening a counter display of bookmarks that had been disrupted from their usual neatness.

"No," Dee prevaricated, a smug expression forming on her young face, "because she was very interested when I told her we had a famous author in residence at the Cove this year, that he lived next door to me and that he was very, very close . . . intimately close with my sister."

"You said what!" Abby choked, her head jerking rapidly to attention.

"Well, you are, aren't you?" Dee stammered, hastily sliding off the stool to put it between herself and her sister for protection.

"Well, you make it sound very, very, crude. V-very—" Abby stuttered uncomfortably.

"I made it sound very romantic," Dee told her matter-of-factly. "Our glamourous reporter was really interested. Maybe she'll want to interview Nick when he comes back. What great publicity! Why, I'll bet they put your pictures in the paper and everything!"

Abby groaned and rubbed her forehead painfully. "Listen, honey, I love you dearly, but you've got to stop—"

"I don't care," Dee interrupted defiantly. "What difference does it make if some passing stranger knows about you and Nick? Everybody in Camden knows. I think it's wonderful that you two are in love."

Abby sighed and shook her head resignedly. "I guess there was no harm done. I doubt the woman was more than just an interested vacationer."

Dee flashed her a wide smile. "You're swell, Abby. Listen, she's probably forgotten everything I said.

119

Who listens to kids anyway, right? And—say, what's in that box?" She stopped, immediately transferring her interest to the large carton sitting on the floor.

Abby chuckled. "Actually, it's a little going-away gift for your trip tomorrow," she drawled in a teasing tone.

"It is! Gosh!" Dee scrambled around the counter and ran over to the carton, ripping open the cardboard sides with all the delight of a child on Christmas morning.

"I'm glad I didn't spend money on gift wrapping," Abby intoned dryly.

"Oh, Abby! It's the suitcase I was telling you about. I love it!"

"I'm glad," her sister echoed humorously. "With all the hints you've been dropping about having to use that old, practically broken suitcase of mine, I'd hate to think I missed your cue."

"This is just great," Dee gushed, trying the zippers on all the pockets and running her fingers over the tan leather bindings that framed the navy blue fabric of the overnight bag. "Mom and John are taking me shopping at three thirty—"

"Which is exactly four minutes from now." Abby grinned, pointing at the wall clock.

"Wow, I better move it." Dee picked up the suitcase, came over and gave her sister a kiss, and skipped out the door, leaving Abby to pick up the torn carton.

Three and a half hours later Abby unlocked the front door of her cottage and blissfully stepped into the cool, quiet interior. An early evening rally of weekend bookbuyers had left her limp and exhausted. She eased off her espadrilles and padded into the kitchen. There, taped on the refrigerator, was a note from her mother. It seemed John was treating her and Dee to dinner after their shopping expedition and Abby would find a casserole that needed only warming in the refrigerator.

Wonderful, Abby grimaced, tossing her purse onto the kitchen table. Just what every girl dreams of—a Friday night all by her lonesome! She looked at the refrigerator door, pulled it open, and then pushed it shut again. She walked over to the back door, opened it, and wandered out onto the porch. She leaned over the thick wooden railing, her lungs greedily sucking in the scent of bracing salt air. The haunting cries of the gulls called to her as did the lazily rolling surf. It was an invitation she could never refuse. A late lunch made it easy to pass up the casserole, at least for a while. Her weary spirit needed a refreshing, revitalizing tumble with the waves.

The door chimes halted Abby's progress to her bedroom for her swimsuit. She traced her steps back through the rattan-furnished living room to pull open the front door.

"A Scotsman bearing paintings," announced a familiar masculine voice with absolutely no trace of a highland burr.

"Well, well, Dr. MacDougal, you finally look the part of a psychiatrist with that beard." Abby grinned, reaching up to playfully tug his trim Vandyke before giving a welcoming hug to an old family friend.

Robert MacDougal stroked his brown whiskers reflectively, his twinkling blue eyes belying his pensive face. "I grew this because I have a deeply rooted Freudian-feature complex and I want to impress the hell out of some colleagues in Europe."

"What's all this about Europe?" she questioned with interest.

"Let me bring in my latest collection of artwork for you to ooh and ahh over." He smiled. "Then I'll give you all my news." Robert passed the six large wrapped canvases over the threshold into Abby's waiting hands.

"You know, I sold the last six you brought in in less than three weeks," she told him as they carefully leaned the paintings against the sofa frame and removed the brown paper. "Oh, Robert, these are better than any you've brought." Abby breathed ecstatically. Indeed, each canvas was alive with color, texture, and feeling only achieved by an accomplished artist. They ran the gamut from seascapes, to still life, to delicate pastoral scenes.

"You are very good for my ego." He grinned.

"You are very good for my business," she parried.

"Say, where's my usual rousing welcome from your bubbly sister and Claire?" Robert inquired, cocking his head, and listening for the others.

"Well, I'm afraid you only get me tonight." Abby smiled. "Dee and Mom are out doing some shopping. Dee's going to the Van Hallston's in Washington tomorrow for a two-week stay with Vicky."

"That's right," he recalled thoughtfully. "I met Vicky when she stayed here last summer. Nice kid."

"The whole family is great," she agreed. "I was really glad that Vicky and Dee remained friends even when her father got transferred. It makes a nice break for Dee to go there this summer. She's been working at the shop too." Abby linked her hand through his arm and together they moved toward the kitchen. "Come on, we can use some lemonade for our Herculean efforts. I want to hear all about this trip to Europe you mentioned."

"I'm leaving early tomorrow for a psychiatrist's convention in Edinburgh," Robert told her with boyish enthusiasm as he settled himself on a kitchen chair. "Then I plan on taking a three-week tour of my ancestral homeland to see how many MacDougals I can locate. I've even been thinking of buying property over there. I retire next year, you know."

Abby turned from the refrigerator, pitcher in hand, to smile at him. Robert MacDougal was about her height, with thick, dark brown hair streaked with gray at the temples. His lean figure, clad in a light blue golf shirt and plaid slacks, only reenforced the image of a man of forty, while he was actually some twenty years older. He had come into their lives four years ago, when her mother had needed therapy. He was more than just a doctor; Robert was a member of the family.

"It's hard for me to imagine you retiring," Abby said thoughtfully, passing him a tall glass of shimmering liquid. "What will you do, turn from psychiatrist into a full-time painter?"

"I think so." He grinned, pausing to take a sip of the refreshing drink. "I've been asked to take an advisory position on the hospital board of Richmond Memorial and I'll keep a few patients whom I don't feel I can shift to another doctor. And of course I'll never miss a medical convention." He grinned rather rakishly.

She laughed and shook her head. "Then why buy retirement property in Scotland? It doesn't sound like you'll be able to use it."

He sighed, studying the square pattern of the floor tiles. "I talk a good line, don't I?" He looked up, his mouth twisting wryly. "You know I could never leave here. There are too many memories." His blue eyes traveled hungrily about the kitchen as if making sure everything was in its proper place.

Abby leaned against the counter, looking at him with compassionate eyes. "It's hard for you to come here, isn't it, Robert?"

He gave her a crooked smile. "Sometimes it is very hard to walk through your front door and not have Emily walk into my arms. You know, I got quite a shock when I saw that short haircut of yours tonight. You could pass for her twin."

She fingered her curls almost apologetically. "Robert, I—"

He laughed and shook his head. "Don't worry about it, honey. We psychiatrists are trained to combat this sort of thing." He finished the rest of his drink, stood up, and shoved his hands into his trouser pockets. "You know I loved your aunt, figuratively and literally. For years we played the same silly game. I'd drive down from Richmond each weekend and we'd spend our three days together like honeymooners—talking, laughing, loving. On occasion we'd take little trips together. Every Sunday evening before I left I'd ask her to marry me. She'd laugh and say, 'Who'd want to be burdened with a middle-aged spinster with a bad heart.' " He looked at Abby, a wealth of emotion in his eyes. "I wanted her. With or without the bad heart. Our weekends were as close to marriage as she would let me get. So—" Robert waved his hand as if clearing the room of unspoken thoughts. "Well, now that you've heard my confession, what's new around here? How's Claire? Is she still helping out in the bookstore?"

Abby nodded. "Mom's doing fine. In fact, I've never seen her so happy and content. And, of course, Dee's doing just wonderfully too."

"And you?" He looked at her, closing one eye and using the other in an imitation of a magnifying glass. "Hmm, I'd say you were wonderful too."

"It shows, does it?" She wrinkled her nose, feeling her cheeks tinge with color, then gave a low laugh. "Yes, I'm wonderful too. I met someone. Someone really special. I'm in love with him, Robert."

He searched her face intently. "And who has worked this miracle?"

"Nick Maxwell. He's a writer who's taken Gull Cottage for the summer. I told him everything," Abby said in a rush before stopping to take a gulp of lemonade.

Robert held his empty glass up in a silent toast. "That was a giant step for you to take."

She nodded. "Nick is so easy to talk to. At first, well, at first I didn't even like him. Gradually we became closer and now . . ." Her voice trailed off and she cleared her throat. "I—I worry that I need him too much. That I'm using him as a crutch."

"Only you know the answer to that question, Abby."

She exhaled slowly, her fingers playing with the gently bobbing ice cubes in her glass. "Maybe we should adjourn to the living room so I could lie on the couch." She grinned ruefully.

"Well, this would be the first time you ever let me help you," Robert commented dryly.

"I guess I've been a rather stubborn, hardheaded little creature, haven't I?"

"Hmm," he agreed and they both laughed.

"I've had so many other things to worry about these last four years, that I couldn't . . . wouldn't take time for myself. I was doing just fine before Nick came. I'll admit my relationships with men were very businesslike. I just wasn't ready to let anyone get close to me."

"Listen," Robert told her quietly, professionally, "it's not unusual for early traumatic relationships to make a person fearful of having other emotional involvements. You had two men hurt you—"

"I know." Abby sighed and rubbed her forehead. "I felt such a failure. A failure at being a daughter and not trying to improve my relationship with my father. A failure as a business student for not recognizing the obvious signs of our financial problems. Then when Eric Dalton began to drift away, I thought I had failed again. This time as a fiancée, as a woman."

"But you didn't fail with Eric," Robert pointed out quickly. "He was nothing more than—"

"A cunning, cheating, lying bastard," she finished.

"I couldn't have said it better myself." He grinned and they both laughed.

"It took a long time, much too long, for me to be able to talk, let alone laugh over Eric." Abby smiled reflectively. "I may have thought I was a worldly wise twenty-one; but in here"—she tapped her chest with her fingers—"the real me was a scared, insecure, naive child.

"The handsome Mr. Dalton just channeled his overabundance of charm in my direction. I lapped it up and let my rose-colored vision do the rest. Eric pampered my fragile young ego, wined and dined me, treated me like the proverbial princess in a fairy tale. I honestly believed he held the glass slipper that would fit my size-nine foot perfectly." She lifted her eyes from their pensive study of the linoleum to gaze into Robert's compassionate face. "What a tragic laugh that Prince Charming fantasy turned out to be. I was so angry. Angry that Eric didn't love me. Angry that he was having an affair with another woman while he was engaged to me. Angry with myself that I wasn't capable of making a man want only me and growing more angry for having let a man make such a fool of me. No one likes to be used; it's very demeaning . . ." Her voice trailed off, bearing traces of sadness that echoed on her attractive features.

"And your Nick Maxwell is . . . ?" Robert prodded, his tone gently guiding her back to the present.

"My Nick Maxwell," Abby continued, her face glowing radiantly with the mention of his name, "is so different. He's honest and frank and natural. We talk about everything. I have no secrets from Nick and he has none from me. There couldn't be two more opposite men in the world than Nick and Eric. Nick is the one person I want to be with when the day is through. If something should happen to him— something physically disabling—I'd still want him, need him, love him."

"It sounds like Nick Maxwell should go into psychiatry. He seems to have done what I could never do for you," Robert commented almost grudgingly.

"Robert, don't feel that way," Abby pleaded, walking over and linking her hand into the crook of his arm.

He gave a self-conscious half-laugh and patted her hand. "Professional jealousy, my dear," he admitted ruefully. "I'm a very proprietorial and protective person where you and your family are concerned. When do I get to meet your man?"

Abby smiled, feeling deeply touched by the depth of Robert's emotional ties. "I only wish you could meet him. He's been in New York all week with his publisher. He finished a new suspense novel that I know is going to be a best seller. It's got the most marvelous plot and he's such a good writer."

"You'd better make sure I get an autographed copy," he warned. "I'm glad to see you so happy," Robert told her earnestly as they wandered out on the back deck to enjoy the ruby glow of the summer sky. "The change in you is wonderful; even if I couldn't work this miracle myself, I'm glad someone else was able to help you. You're a wonderful woman, Abby. So warm, so loving, you're very easy to fall in love with. Hey, why the tears?" He pulled her chin up to gaze into her liquid gray eyes.

"I guess I'm crying for all the time I lost. If I had let you . . ."

He slid a comforting arm around her shoulder, pressing her close against his side. "Don't ever cry over the past. Look toward the future. Your future looks as brilliant as tonight's sunset."

"Robert, I love you," she sniffed. "Are you sure you have to be gone so long?"

He looked at the gold watch on his wrist and gave a reluctant sigh. "As a matter of fact I've got to head back to Richmond right now. As usual I left all the packing for the last minute. You'd think a psychiatrist would be better organized. Of course, that could signify some latent—"

"Robert!" Abby groaned in mock agony. "Mom and Dee should be home soon," she coaxed hopefully.

"No, I really can't." He shook his head and turned to go back into the house. "I really have to get moving. I was wondering if you could do me one rather large favor though."

"Just ask."

He slid his hand into his breast pocket. "Here's an extra key to my apartment. Six more of my paintings are on display at the Caufield Gallery. Ronald Caufield is going to leave whichever ones don't sell in my apartment. If you could go and pick them up after these six are sold—"

"No problem," Abby told him, taking the key and dropping it into her purse, lying on the kitchen table. "Let me write out a check to cover the paintings I've sold. It will help in the rate of exchange when you hit Scotland."

"How are you doing with your computer fight with Charge-X?" Robert grinned, watching her fill out a check for a very impressive amount.

She looked up from writing and grimaced. "I thought for a while I was winning. I figured the repunched data cards would cause some trouble and hopefully a real person would investigate and find all the letters I wrote. You've got to admit I did send the proper cancellation notices."

Robert smiled. "That's true. You've been more than fair."

"I thought so," she agreed. "But two weeks ago I got another one of their threatening computer letters. Yesterday, however, I mailed their data card back in such a way that it will definitely get noticed." Abby grinned wickedly. "I did exactly what they told me not to do to their precious card. I folded, spindled, and mutilated the damn thing!"

Robert's laughter echoed through the house. "You ought to get together and compare notes with Ronald Caufield," he told her.

"What happened to him" Abby asked interestedly.

"He tried to use an automatic teller. You know,

one of those computer terminals activated by a plastic access card. He punched in his personal identification number and waited for his fifty dollars. The darn machine kept spitting out fifty dollar packets and refused to return his card."

She rubbed her forehead and shook her head. "What did he do?"

"Ron made the mistake of kicking the darn thing and it triggered a silent alarm. Then he found himself surrounded by police cars."

Abby grunted in disgust. "Man versus machine. It's not a pleasant confrontation. I've had a lot of people tell me about billing problems on their credit card statements. And you know how long the fight with food and beverage dispensers has been going on. You plug in one of those metal monsters and they really seem to acquire a mind of their own. They take your money but eat or drink your request themselves." She sighed and passed him his check. The only thing I do worry about are the dunning letters I get from Charge-X. I realize the police won't be surrounding my store but—"

"You might have to end up getting a lawyer to settle this for you," Robert advised her thoughtfully.

"You might be right," Abby conceded, walking with him slowly toward the front door. "It's going to be a long time before we see you again," she said sadly.

"I'll bring you something nice from the Highlands," he bantered lightly. "I was thinking of a Scotsman, but—"

Abby laughed. She bit her lip and gave him a hard,

affectionate hug. A lump of emotion was still constricting her throat long after the red taillights of Robert MacDougal's blue MG melted into the hazy twilight. The cottage felt very empty and Abby felt terribly alone. With a determined shake of her head she went into her small bedroom and pulled on her old white two-piece bathing suit. She stopped in the kitchen long enough to pop one of her mother's mouthwatering ham and noodle casseroles into the oven and set the automatic controls so that if her swim lasted longer than thirty minutes, the oven would keep her dinner warm.

CHAPTER TEN

Abby stopped long enough to grab her yellow surf rider from the back porch before scampering across the hard-packed sand that was peppered with tiny sea shells. She plunged into the building evening surf, jumping over the waves until she was waist deep in the warm water. Except for a handful of gulls and an anchored trawler, she was the ocean's only visitor. The beach was deserted, its usual frolickers abandoning it for the glitter of a Friday evening at one of Virginia Beach's many night spots.

Well, Abby smiled, she'd let the sea be her date for tonight. Wriggling onto the rider, she waited for the next breaker. The strong riptide pulled the float sideways and a solid wall of water propelled her forward. She rode the crest of the wave until it turned into a rolling line of frothy ruffles, letting her knees and hands scrape the bottom of the shore.

She flipped her body over to lie face up on the rider, letting the waves gently rock her while she studied the sky. A bank of fluffy white clouds had covered the sun. Its powerful rays edging them with silver and streaking the sky with strips of coral. The salt spray was forming a heavy mist on the horizon, giving an orchid cast to the darkening blue haze of her solitary world.

Abby wondered what Nick was doing. Perhaps he was watching the sunset, wishing he was back at the Cove. Perhaps he was thinking about her, as she constantly thought about him. She remembered their last night together. He had walked her to her front door, his lips kissing the tiny scar on her wrist, his eyes more eloquent than words.

His image was indelibly impressed on her mind. The sound of his deep voice, the scent of his cologne, and the warmth of his hard, muscular body were potent enough to rekindle the flames of passion that seared her veins.

For the past week she had persistently tried to replace his image with paperwork. She had even managed to get a month ahead in some areas; but, relentlessly, especially when she was in bed at night, Nick's face stepped in front of her mind's eye with stunning clarity. "Come home fast, love," she whispered achingly to the darkening sky.

When the waves once again beached her float, Abby reluctantly got to her feet, shook out her hair, and slowly wandered back along the sand. She squinted into the distance, her breath catching as she recognized a tall familiar figure clad in white swim trunks heading in her direction. Even in the gray twilight, she knew that broad-shouldered physique and self-assured walk could belong to only one man.

"Nick!" her voice yelled, she ran as if wings had grown on her feet. "Why didn't you come up to the house? I've been waiting for you," she stammered breathlessly, her voice caught in her throat, sensing an unaccustomed harshness about his face and noting the rigid stance.

"Oh, I went up to your house," came a voice she barely recognized, a voice filled with anger and bitterness. "Only you were entertaining."

Abby exhaled in relief. "That was—"

"I don't want to know who he is," Nick interrupted savagely. "I don't get it. I honestly don't get it. I thought we had something strong going for us."

"What . . . what are you talking about." She put a hand on his bare shoulder only to have him roughly step away as if he'd been burnt. They just stared at each other as if across a dark chasm—Abby's face a confused and puzzled visage, Nick's a savagely twisted countenance.

"You have the gall to ask that. I heard every word you two said on the porch," he returned, his voice loaded with contempt. "The change in you was wonderful. He didn't mind if it took someone else to bring it about. How wonderful you are, how bright, how warm, how easy you were to fall in love with." Each word came out slower and harsher than its predecessor. "I was gone seven days—one lousy week, worried the whole time over whether someone else would try to take away the one woman I care most about. And I came home to find out that's exactly what happened!"

"But, Nick," she protested, watching his knuckles tighten as his hands gripped the white towel draped around his neck.

"My sense of who I was always seemed to be based on my work, my achievements. Then I met you and somehow all that didn't matter." His rough voice rudely overrode her attempt to explain. He raked his damp hair with a shaky hand, trying to control this unusually violent feeling that threatened to overpower him. "I'm afraid I found I need you more than you need me. I pretended you needed me. But I can see how wrong I was. All week long I was thinking about you, very much afraid that I wasn't man enough to keep the new you happy. I can see I won't have to worry about that anymore. What a fool I was." His chest was heaving, his breathing as rapid as if he'd run a marathon.

Abby stared at Nick, her entire being almost bursting with the joy of knowing, of actually hearing how much he cared for her. "Will you listen!" she exploded, her foot stamping the wet sand angrily. "You are right, Nick Maxwell, you are a fool! If you had walked up on the back porch instead of skulking in the shadows, you would have been introduced to Robert MacDougal, Dr. Robert MacDougal, my mother's psychiatrist." She pushed her hands hard against his bare chest. "My Aunt Emily's lover—not mine. A man who is going to retire next year . . ." She pushed harder, forcing him backward into the ankle deep tide. "We weren't talking about him and me, we were talking about you and me . . . about how much I love you and missed you and . . . and . . ." She paused, swallowing hard. Abby put all the strength of her five-foot-ten-inch, one-hundred-forty-pound body into a might shove that sent a very surprised Nick Maxwell flailing into the surf. "And that's for calling me only once all week, you r-rat!" she stammered. Clinging to her newfound anger, she turned and ran back up the beach.

She managed to get only three yards before she was pulled down on the sand and flipped over, Nick's powerful body lying astride her own. "Abby, if you're lying to me, I don't want to know it." His voice was low and strained.

She slid her hands around his neck, pulling his head down, holding him against her with all her strength. "Nick, I love you so much it hurts. I've missed you horribly this past week. How could you ever think—"

His mouth fiercely closed over hers, parting her soft lips with a savage urgency that caused her to utter a throaty moan of pain. She was suddenly a whole person again, feeling the hard, muscular length of his body press intimately against her soft form, reveling in the tender caresses of his skilled hands and the soft murmurings of love from his lips.

"Why did you only call that once?" she asked, feeling secure and content in his arms.

"Talking to you on the phone was pure hell," he told her thickly, his teeth nipping the sensitive cord of her neck. "All I got to hold was a cold, plastic telephone receiver. My mind was vividly remembering the scent of your perfume, the sweetness of your mouth, the way your body curves so perfectly into mine. I love you, Abby."

"I've waited so long to hear you say that." Her voice was like a sob. Her fingers gently traced the strong contours of his face to linger against his lips. "Oh, Nick . . . Nick." She kissed the cleft of his chin, burrowing her face against the curve of his neck. Her tongue tasted the salty residue clinging to his earlobe from his ocean swim.

"Abby." He pulled slightly away. "Abby, I've got to tell you something.

"What?" she whispered, pressing herself closer to his warm body.

"Listen, this is important." He swallowed hard, determined to be totally honest with her. "My name —it isn't Nick."

"Hmm . . ." She looked up at him, her eyes glowing like diamonds. A smile twitched at the corners of her mouth. "What is it?" she teased, running her hands across the taut muscles of his shoulders. "Nicholas? Nichols? Nickolai? I know." She laughed, her arms sliding around his neck. "It's Rumpelstiltskin." She laughed and kissed his nose.

"No. Abby listen, I really should have told you this from the beginning." His voice was serious, he pulled her hands from his neck. "It's Dominick." He took a deep breath. "Dominick Maxwell—"

"A rose by any other name," she interrupted lightly. "I can still call you Nick, can't I? I'll use Dominick when I'm really angry . . . but I'm not angry now." Her voice was low and seductive in his ear.

"I've missed you so this week and I can certainly think of better things to do than talk." Fiercely her hands cupped his face, pulling his mouth down to her parted lips in a hungry kiss.

Nick gave a low murmur of surprise, his muscular body pressing her farther into the sand, taking over control. His hard tongue probed the moist sweetness of her mouth, his hands slowly caressing the swelling curves of her breasts before his fingers deftly disposed of the top of her bathing suit. She sighed, nuzzling her cheek against his jaw. His skin was warm and smelled of salt mixed with the spicy scent of his cologne. Her own body felt boneless beneath his exploring hands. Her mind floated on a sea of pleasurable sensations, her own passion mounting with such a force that it made her tremble with a mixture of fear and excitement.

A soft moan of pleasure escaped her lips when Nick's mouth followed the curve of her swelling breasts, his beard-roughened cheek gently resting in the scented valley. His muscular thigh slid intimately between her long legs, the clinging wet swim trunks leaving no doubt of the extent of his desire.

The slow, sweet arousal of her body under his masterly tutelage was an all-consuming flame that overrode her mind and made rational thinking impossible. Her heightened senses ached for complete possession, and with that came her final surrender. "Make love to me, Nick," she whispered, her fingers lovingly tangled in the dark curly hairs of his chest.

He lifted his head from the soft pillow of her breasts. "Abby, you've never—"

"I know. But I love you." There was no need to moralize, just the all-consuming desire to be with him as a woman, to love him in the fullest possible sense—for them to finally become one.

"I love you, you know that. You can feel how much I want you. Not here, not like this." The ache in his voice belied his words.

Abby smiled at him, his face so clear and so close. She turned her head slightly to the scene beyond. This is the perfect place, she thought, where heaven meets earth in a seemingly never-ending horizon. At their feet were the waters of the sea that had kissed many distant shores; their canopy was a blue-black sky alight with a dusting of brilliant stars that rivaled the glowing moon. "This is the perfect place." Her lips whispered her words of consent against his firm mouth.

"Abby." Her name emerged almost as a groan from deep within his throat. His arms lifted her soft, pliant body on top of him, his hands slowly following the curves of her waist and hips pressing her intimately against burgeoning passion. She arched her throat, his lips blazing a trail of fire along the soft skin of her shoulder and neck. The bottom of her damp bathing suit twisted roughly down her thighs, he rolled her onto her back, the soft white sand yielding under their weight. Her body arched instinctively beneath him, aching with a hungry passion that sent a shiver through her veins.

She let her hands drift down his chest and over his stomach, her fingers sliding under the waistband of his white bathing trunks—fingers that seemed to be guided by hidden sensual longings that this man ignited. His warm breath once again filled her mouth —his lips hard and possessive, savagely absorbing her very life's breath into his body. His hand strayed over her abdomen to probe the soft skin of her inner thigh.

The unmistakable sound of tires on gravel penetrated the intimate world they had lost themselves in. "Damn," Nick swore hoarsely, as the glare of headlights swept across the cliff above them and a car came to a halt in the driveway of her cottage.

His breathing was ragged, his body lying across hers like a shield. Abby swallowed the bitter lump of emotion caught in her throat. She felt sad; more than anything else she had wanted to become a part of Nick tonight. He felt her shiver and pulled her against his chest, wrapping his arms around her trembling body, his hands gently cradling the soft, full breasts his lips had just tasted. She turned her head and moved it, almost shyly, against his chest. The pounding of his heart was oddly comforting in her ear. He looked down into her flushed face, so clearly visible in the moonlight, and pulled her even closer to his side, brushing the sand from her back with a gentle hand, letting their minds regain control of their heightened senses.

After a few minutes Abby sat up and shakily replaced her swimsuit. Arms locked around each other's waist, they walked slowly, silently, up the steep embankment to the back steps of her now brightly lit cottage.

The pressure of Nick's hand halted their progress.

"Maybe their return was fate. I want to spend more than a few stolen minutes making love to you," he said in a deep emotion filled voice. "I still have conversations to finish with you; but you seem to be expert at making me lose my powers of concentration." He slanted her a crooked grin.

"Strange, you're the only one I've ever had that effect on." Abby fluttered her eyelashes at him in theatrical fashion. They were both still laughing when they entered the kitchen.

"Look who I discovered on the beach," Abby announced as the back door slammed shut behind them.

"Hey, welcome home, son." John grinned at the couple. "Everything straightened out in New York?" He arched an inquisitive gray brow.

"Worked out perfectly." Nick nodded, lounging against the counter with Abby still held to his side. "All the little details were easier to iron out than I expected," he continued cryptically. Father and son both smiled at each other.

"My, God," she groaned in a low voice near his ear, "I forgot to ask how your publisher liked the manuscript."

His hand gave her waist a reassuring squeeze. "Everything went fine. I may have a little rewriting to do, but the editor will get back to me."

Dee literally ran into the room waving handfuls of shopping bags, her mother following at a more sedate pace. "Abby, wait until you see all the neat things I got on sale. We saw the paintings. Robert was here, wasn't he? Is he coming back? I hate to miss him." Dee's lungs paused for air. She grinned at her sister and winked. "Hi, Nick. I'm really glad you're back. Abby's been working herself to death again."

Abby shook her head in mock annoyance. "Why don't you just put on a little fashion show for us. That should keep you out of trouble for a while. Mom, Robert's on his way to a medical convention in Edinburgh," she added for Claire's benefit.

"That's wonderful." Claire smiled. "He's always wanted to visit Scotland. Hello, Nick, I'm glad everything went so well."

"Just who is this mysterious Robert," John interrupted, watching Claire intently as she edged passed him toward the stove.

"Oh, he's just a friend of my late sister's. He does most of the paintings that Abby displays in the bookshop," she said in a casual voice. She pulled open the oven door and frowned. "Oh, dear. Abby, I'm afraid the casserole has crusted over."

"Don't worry about it, Mom," Abby told her lightly. "I guess my . . . swim took longer than I expected." She could feel the heat of color stain her cheeks as Nick's eyes found hers.

"Why don't you sit down." Claire bustled about the room, pulling out dishes, silverware, and glasses. "Nick, you want some dinner, don't you? Why don't you tell us all about your trip?"

"I'm going to try on my new outfit," Dee called, disappearing into her bedroom.

Abby and Nick slid into adjoining chairs, Abby's smooth silken leg intertwining with Nick's muscular hair-roughened one under the table while they listened to their respective parent's chatterings.

Hours later Abby was surprised to hear a knock on her bedroom door. It was her mother, in a light cotton robe obviously thrown hastily over a sea green nylon gown, her hair matted and twisted by agitated fingers.

Abby hastily pushed aside the checkbook she'd been balancing and scrambled out of bed. "What's the matter, Mom? Are you sick? Is it Dee?"

"No." Claire's hands fluttered nervously against her throat. "It's me. I'm not sick, just . . . I can't sleep," she sighed and rubbed her forehead. "Abby, I suppose you thought it was very strange of me not to tell John who Robert was."

"Well," Abby commented thoughtfully, "you did evade his question by suddenly turning into the perfect hostess."

"Oh, and I thought I did that so cleverly." Her mother's mouth drooped at the corners.

"Say, what's this all about?"

"Well, I haven't told John yet about . . . about things." Claire cleared her throat, deliberately avoiding her daughter's eyes. "The proper time just hasn't come up. And . . . and lots of people still think *psychiatrist* is a dirty word."

Abby laughed in relief and took her mother's clammy hands, pulling her down to sit on the narrow bed. "These days most people preface a conversation with 'my analyst said,' " she told her quietly. "Psychiatrist and therapy are not dirty words. That's what the doctors are there for—to help people who cannot help themselves at a particular point of time in their lives. Major businesses have psychiatrists available for their employees, politicians have admitted to therapy. And practically everyone in Hollywood has at least one analyst." She grinned, her hand tipping up her mother's face. "I don't think John's the type of person who would think the lesser of you for getting help," she added gently.

"You really believe that?"

"Yes. Nick wasn't. He knows."

Claire looked up and blinked. "He does?"

Abby nodded. "He's known about everything for a long time. It didn't matter. I know you'll find the same reaction with his father."

"John's offered to drive Dee and me to Washington tomorrow."

"That was nice of him," Abby said slowly, watching her mother's pale cheeks suddenly flame.

"Well, he said he had friends there himself and it isn't that far a drive." She coughed and let her fingers trace the yellow daisies on the bedsheets.

"You're getting very fond of John aren't you, Mom?"

"Well." Claire cleared her throat. "He's nice. A little pushy in the kitchen." Her lips twisted wryly. Suddenly both she and Abby were laughing like two high-school girls sharing hidden secrets.

"I suppose you think it's silly for a woman my age—"

Abby pressed her fingers over her mother's lips. "I don't think it's silly for a woman of any age to fall in love. And you are in love with John." It was a statement, not a question, and was answered by her mother's slow nod.

"I'm afraid to tell him about our past and I'm worried because he said he has things to discuss with me. Do you suppose Nick told him?" she asked anxiously.

Abby fingered the collar of her red-and-pink striped nightshirt thoughtfully. "No. I think Nick would leave the telling to you. Maybe John wants to tell you about his life, his late wife, his business. You know, we don't even know what he's retired from." She smiled at her mother.

"You think that's what it is?" Claire seemed to find reassurance in her daughter's affirmative nod. "You aren't going to mind if we're gone an extra day or two, are you?"

"No, as a matter of fact," Abby said lightly, grimacing as she felt a tell-tale blush stain her own cheeks. "Nick and I could use a few days alone. We've got things to discuss ourselves."

Claire patted her daughter's hand. "You're very much in love with him, aren't you, dear."

"Yes," Abby told her, "this time it's honest and real and shared."

CHAPTER ELEVEN

"A little to the left," Abby instructed. "No, Nick, my left your right. Now you've got it crooked," she groaned, her voice filled with mock annoyance, her lips twitching with amusement. "I thought you were good with your hands."

Nick straightened from a rather precarious position on the open balcony. "I didn't hear any complaints last night," he drawled, waving his hammer threateningly. "Picture-hanging is not one of my many attributes." He kneeled and reached down to adjust a wire he had wrapped around one of the wrought iron balcony rails, sliding one of Robert MacDougal's canvases over to his right. "How's that?"

"Perfect." She grinned. "You've got only five more to go."

"Wonderful." Nick raised his eyes heavenward. "I

can think of better ways to spend a Saturday morning." He grinned wickedly, letting his brown eyes roam leisurely over Abby's figure.

She clasped a hand to the square neck of her madras plaid sundress in feigned consternation. "I don't know that I have a thing to fear. As a matter of fact, I think we have a role-reversal problem," she teased. "You seem to be playing the shy, frightened virgin while I'm the lecherous rogue."

He threw his head back and gave a deep hearty laugh. "Wait until tonight, when we are finally all alone. I've got two houses to chase you through," he warned, a lazy smile curving his mouth.

"Promises, promises," she caroled baitingly, but even from a distance Abby felt her breath quicken under Nick's intoxicating gaze and the impending promise of that evening.

"Never mind, I'll disregard your pleas for mercy tonight." He cleared his throat, sounding very serious. "Abby, we've got to get a few important things talked about—"

"Save it for tonight, Nick, or I'll think you just want to get out of hanging the rest of these paintings," she interrupted gaily, climbing up a few steps to hand him another canvas. "Besides, it's time to open the shop."

Abby unbolted the front door and picked up the early morning mail from the postman. She quickly sorted through the numerous book catalogs, circulars, and magazines, when a very official-looking white envelope caught her eye. It was from Charge-X.

Slowly she walked to the register, staring at the printed return address with mounting trepidation. It wasn't one of their regular orange-and-white banded envelopes their computer warning notices usually arrived in. Those had always been addressed to the bookshop; this was addressed to her. A stark, authoratative envelope, almost legal in its appearance. Abby exhaled slowly, catching her lower lip between white teeth, her mind trying to recall their last warning letter. They had mentioned legal action, but what on earth could they do to her?"

"Hey, Abby, is anything the matter?"

She looked up and found Nick watching her. He was much too observant and astute, she thought wryly. She looked down at the envelope. Well, nothing was going to spoil her day or her night! Nothing, least of all Charge-X. "It's just another circular from a calendar company," she lied, her voice betraying none of the alarm signals her brain kept sending. "I think I ordered a bit too soon." She reached behind the counter, pulled open a drawer, and shoved all the mail out of sight and, hopefully, out of mind. She'd tell Nick about it later. Maybe he could figure out a way to get Charge-X off her back.

"I'll bring in the last two paintings from the car. Will you keep an eye on things here for a minute?"

"Sure, can you get them all right?"

"No problem, besides, I left the keys in the ignition and my purse on the front seat, though I'm the only one who uses that alley."

"Here I thought you were the perfect business-woman," he teased.

149

"You've proved to be a disruptive influence around here, Mr. Maxwell," she retorted spiritedly before disappearing out the rear door.

Nick was carefully attaching wires to the back of another picture frame when he heard the tiny bell on the front door announce the shop's first customer of the day.

"Well, well," drawled a seductive, feminine voice, "this is a new role for you, Dominick."

His tongue wet suddenly parched lips, his hands slowly lowering the canvas that had been shielding his face. He looked down through the railings and found the voice had a three-dimensional body attached to it. The image of Marie Reynolds came sharply into focus.

She removed a pair of oversize sunglasses and smiled up at him—a thin, shallow smile that was more like a sneer. Her eyes, even from a distance, glittered like black onyx. "How fast the mighty have fallen. From company president and best-selling author to picture hanger." Her pink tongue clicked against thirty-two perfect white teeth.

"What the hell are you doing here, Marie?" Nick's voice was harsh and rude. "It's a long way from Fifth Avenue."

She picked an imaginary bit of lint off the neckline of her white designer bouclé-knit dress, readjusting the narrow red reptile belt that emphasized her tiny waist. "Let's just say we have some unfinished business with each other." She smiled sweetly up at him.

"What the devil are you talking about?" he asked

150

roughly, putting down the tack hammer he was still gripping and eyeing her sharply.

"I told you before you left New York that I wasn't through with you. No man ever brushes me off the way you did," she told him in a deadly low voice, her eyes glittering maliciously. "I don't forget or forgive."

"You know damn well there was nothing between us. You used me. I used you. That was the extent of our so-called relationship," Nick stated evenly.

"But I wasn't through using you," Marie hissed at him. She stopped and cleared her throat. "I thought I'd take a little vacation, enjoy the seaside. Check out your latest acquisition. Didn't your darling Miss Wetherby tell you I was in her shop yesterday?"

"You . . . you talked to Abby?" He went cold, beads of perspiration forming on his forehead and hands. His palms were slippery as they gripped the iron railing.

"No," she answered, studying the long red lacquered tips of her fingers with contrived interest, "but her sister was a wealth of knowledge."

"Dee?" His dark brows pulled together in puzzlement.

"Yes, she's a veritable chatterbox where her sister and you are concerned," Marie continued blithely. "You seem to have accomplished quite a lot in four weeks, Dominick. A new book, which to paraphrase the younger Miss Wetherby, is absolutely fantastic, a real blockbuster; and, of course, there's your umm . . . intimate affair with the elder Miss Wetherby."

"Abby and I are not having an affair," Nick stated firmly, not liking the derogatory allegation.

"Of course you're not," she agreed sweetly. She walked over to the base of the staircase and looked up at him. "You love her, don't you? Abby means a lot to you, doesn't she?" Marie's control slipped, the shrillness in her voice betraying her emotions.

"Yes."

It was the sincerity of that one word that ignited the blonde's fury. "Why her? Why not me? What makes her so special? What did you find in her that was missing in me?" she demanded, her small breasts angrily rising and falling under the clingy material of her dress.

"I don't know how to explain it to you—"

"My God, she's not even beautiful. She's nothing compared to me," Marie interrupted harshly.

Nick's jaw hardened. "Your beauty is only skin deep."

"Skin deep was good enough for you once," she retorted sarcastically.

"God, I don't know how I could have ever gotten involved with you. I must have been crazy. We're not getting anywhere on this merry-go-round," he told her tersely. "How did you find out where I was?"

"Bill York told me all about the little problem Charge-X was having with a Miss Abigail Wetherby. About how you were going to take care of her personally. Ruin her, I think you told him," Marie swept on sadistically, raising her voice when a flash of madras caught her eye.

"Why the hell would York tell you something like that?"

"Dominick, you remember how verbal a man can get in a horizontal position," Marie returned sweetly. "I seldom have trouble getting any kind of information I desire. No matter who has it, no matter how private it is." She picked up the latest hardcover best seller from a display counter. "You know, Dom. This place is a gold mine. I've checked it out. Sales are at a peak and all those rare books upstairs are a little bonus. I think it was very clever of you to come down here and handle the problem yourself. You're not just a talented author and a clever businessman, but a cunning, consummate actor as well. You've got Abby thoroughly convinced you're in love with her. I can see the headlines in the financial section now: DOMINICK MAXWELL BENNETT, PRESIDENT OF CHARGE-X, ACQUIRES PROSPEROUS BOOKSHOP WHILE ON VACATION IN VIRGINIA!" Her voice was clear and triumphant with revenge. She turned the full force of the sadistic delight glittering in her dark eyes on Abby's rigid figure that stood frozen in the alcove.

"What the hell are you trying to do, Marie?" Nick snarled, then he, too, saw Abby, her complexion unnaturally pale, her gray eyes wide with shock.

As he lunged to his feet, Nick's shoe caught the metal head of the hammer, sending it somersaulting through the air. It hit the linoleum with the shattering force of a gunshot, sending a shower of tile fragments splintering across the floor.

Abby felt herself drawing away, shrinking from

within. A time portal opened within her mind, vividly replaying a similar sound from the past. She saw herself walking through the front door of her house in Chicago, clad in a white tennis outfit and swinging her metal racquet.

She heard that same sound—a shot! She dropped the racquet, grabbed a fireplace poker, and ran into her father's study, ready to battle any burglar. But there was no robber—only her father slumped over his desk, a desk littered with bills and credit cards. She reached out, trying to find a pulse, only to come away with blood-stained hands.

"Abby!" Nick's voice sharply pulled her back from the terrifying, morbid journey her mind had taken. "Abby, listen to me. Let me explain." He had hurriedly run down the stairs, trying to take control of the situation.

"Who are you?" Abby asked him in a thin, scared voice.

"He's the president of Charge-X," Marie taunted, stepping between the two of them. "Tell her, Dominick. I'm not lying."

"Wait a minute—" he interrupted, reaching out a hand to Abby, only to have Marie push his arm aside.

"This must be very upsetting for you." Marie gave Abby her most cloying smile. She slid a possessive hand across Nick's chest, her pointed red nails digging through the thin material of his shirt like the tenacious claws of a cat. "Finding out you've been used is very demoralizing. No one likes to be used then tossed away."

"Shut up, Marie," Nick snarled, his fingers cruelly closing around her tiny wrist, pulling the talons loose from his shirt.

"I'm not going to shut up," she hissed, her voice spitting with venom. "Abby must realize how much you mean to me, how intimate we are. We were inseparable while Dominick was in New York. Only business could keep us apart."

"Damn you, Marie, isn't there one ounce of decency in you." He inhaled savagely, his hands gripping her shoulders to move her out of his way.

Abby squeezed her eyes shut against the shooting, blinding pain that knifed through the back of her head. Images in her mind took precedence over the flesh and blood people in the room. Dimly she was aware of arguing voices, but they seemed to be echoing a verbal nightmare of the past.

When her eyes opened, they focused on a man whose face embodied the features of her past deceivers. Abby's lacerated emotions registered the grotesquely twisted images of her father and Eric Dalton. Nick Maxwell had completed an elite triumvirate of cunning illusionists that seemed bent on destroying her life.

"Abby." Nick's voice cracked with strain. He put out a hand and caught her arm. She shook it off and stepped back. "Abby, for God's sake listen to me, let me explain."

"Explain." Her voice was shrill, her eyes like steel chips inside her drawn, white face. "Everything she said is true, isn't it? You are the president of Charge-

X, aren't you? What more could you possibly explain?"

"I did not do this deliberately," he said forcefully. "You've got to believe me. I—"

"Believe you!" Abby spat, looking at Nick with utter contempt. "You must think I'm the most gullible, stupid creature alive. You could win an Academy Award for your performance. You know all the right words, all the right moves, all the right caresses. You made me feel secure and loved when all the while you were waiting for the final kill. Just how long was this deception supposed to last?"

Nick licked his lips nervously and swallowed. He had to choose his words carefully. It was the most important thing in the world for him to convince Abby that his whole charade was not done with an evil intent, that he never meant to hurt her. But he hesitated too long.

"Let me supply the answers for you." Abby's voice was cold, almost indifferent. She drew herself up to her full height and with courage born of raw nerves, challenged him. "You came here with the express purpose of trying to take this bookshop from me, to make an example of me. This was just another crumb for Charge-X to devour under some fine point of the law." Her hand came up to stop his words. "And what was I? Just a little side bonus? A little hors d'oeuvre to snack on while your entree rested until you returned to New York? I'm sure I was no end to your entertainment. This whole scheme was the ultimate joke." Abby's eyes looked at the malicious amusement on Marie Reynolds's face. "How you both must have laughed together over this. I made it so very easy for you."

"Please, Abby," Nick pleaded, stepping closer to her. "You've got to—"

"Got to what?" she spat savagely. "Listen to more lies from you? More tales of love from *her*? God, just looking at the two of you makes me sick." Her lips curled in disgust. "I hate and despise you, Mr. Bennett."

Nick reeled from words that dealt more cruel strength than any physical blow could ever deliver. "Abby, please."

"There's nothing you can say that I want to hear." Abby began to tremble from the mental anguish this couple had induced. Her head was throbbing painfully and her stomach churned to the point of nausea. Her voice rose from the aching void that was her chest. "It doesn't matter. Nothing matters anymore. I'm leaving. This is all you wanted—you've succeeded. It's yours." She turned, her wobbly legs finding the strength to stumble out into the back alley. She yanked open the car door, tossed her purse into the passenger's seat, and slid behind the wheel. The engine roared to life and she reversed recklessly out of the alley without even checking for oncoming traffic. Shifting into drive, Abby pressed the accelerator to the floor. Her eight-year-old Toyota shot forward with the speed of a race car coming out of a pit stop.

"Why did you do that? Couldn't you have found a way of hurting me without hurting Abby?" Nick said quietly, his closed fist hitting the side of the counter in desperation.

"I told you before, I'm the one that calls it quits." Marie stared at him with undisguised hatred. "You left me in New York to face everyone alone. They expected to see us together. Now that you're alone, I'd say the score was even." Her lips thinned into a self-satisfied smile. She opened her red leather purse, extracting a set of car keys. When she looked up, icy anger had etched Nick's face into harsh, taut lines that caused her to quickly back away in fear.

"No one means a damn to you, do they? All you think about is yourself. You're nothing but a shell, a beautiful shell with a rotted soul. You're sick, Marie, sick and ugly. Get the hell out of my sight, you lying bit—" But before he could finish, she had fled.

Nick stood alone in the center of the bookshop staring into space. He prayed that Abby would be all right, that she would come back. He would make her understand. The anguish and confusion she must be feeling were reflected on his own bleak features.

An invisible hand guided the little green Toyota, helping it negotiate the winding curves of the highway that paralleled the Atlantic Ocean. Its driver was half-blinded by tears. The blazing sun glaring off the windshield hammered her eyes into slits and only succeeded in aggravating the throbbing in her head until Abby had no choice but to pull the car off into one of the many shaded rest areas that lined the route.

She turned off the engine and slumped over the steering wheel, letting her burning eyelids release a flood of tears. When she could cry no more, she forced her lungs to take in deep gulps of air. Leaning back against the seat, she pressed a shaky hand against her churning stomach. Her headache seemed to reverberate throughout her entire body.

She was painfully confused. She forced herself to reach out and take control. She had to relive the events that had shattered the morning.

Methodically, she recreated the past hour. She had left the shop and gone out to get the last two paintings from the back of her small station wagon. The canvases had been very unwieldy, forcing her to take them one at a time. When she finally managed to get them into the shop, she heard voices. Thinking it was a customer, she had teasingly hid in the alcove, waiting to see how Nick would handle things.

She pressed trembling fingers to her pounding temples. Things began to get fuzzy, and Abby exhaled slowly, licking her dry lips. She had recognized the woman talking to Nick almost immediately. She was the one who had asked Dee so many questions just the day before, the one Dee had thought was a reporter.

The woman—Marie, Nick had called her—was talking not about an interview but about Charge-X. She wasn't calling him Nick Maxwell but Dominick . . . Dominick Maxwell Bennett, the President of Charge-X, a man who had come to ruin her, seduce her, take over her bookshop. Then there had been that gunshot.

Abby shook her head. No, no one had a gun. That shot was a long time ago, wasn't it? The pain in her head mounted to terrifying proportions. She squeezed her eyes closed, trying to hold back the blackness that threatened to render her unconscious.

Words, people, and events were tumbling about her mind in disjointed confusion. It was impossible for her to remember what had been said or who had said it. The past had transposed itself onto the present.

Panic welled up in her throat. "My God," she cried out loud, "I'm losing my mind." Abby was shaking to such a degree that she became physically ill. She pulled open the car door and ran to a small clump of bushes. She tripped over a tree root and fell on all fours, like a sick animal, retching miserably for some time. When the spasms finally subsided, she sat back against the trunk of a tree, letting the insides of her shivering, limp body settle back into place.

She was four years older and none the wiser. Eric Dalton had been able to fool her. He had been willing to make her his wife, to use her as a stepping stone to a business empire, an empire that was rotting and crumbling under her father's fraudulent control.

Nick had humiliated her even further. He had never mentioned marriage. He had planned on taking her business. And, like a trophy to satisfy his male ego, he would take her body.

Nick was the consummate actor. He had given her false hopes of the future. He had seemed so honest and loving, while all the time he had another woman keeping his bed warm. Just the thought of how she had begged him to make love to her the previous night made her gag.

Was she forever destined to live in a purgatory where fate kept replaying new episodes of the past as perpetual punishment? Was that old curse of the sins of the father doomed to make her life a hell?

Now she had lost a business on some minute legal technicality that she didn't even understand. Her head wearily dropped into her hands. She had to get control of herself before her own mind destroyed her. She couldn't go back to Camden. Nick would be there with that woman and she wasn't strong enough to face them again. She shivered and crawled to her feet, unsteadily heading back to her car. She had to get away.

She slid into the black bucket seat and pulled open her straw handbag. She yanked out her wallet, dumping all the bills and change onto the passenger's seat. She carefully counted the money down to the lint-covered penny she found glued to a half-melted breath mint. The total was a sparse $28.63. That wouldn't even get her a hotel room! Her checkbook. Her fingers hastily sorted through the bag. Irritated, she turned it upside down—comb, compact, lipstick, tissues, address book, pen—but the checkbook was . . . She sighed. The damn checkbook was sitting on her nightstand where she had left it.

A strangled note of hysteria crept out of Abby's throat. If she had possessed a Charge-X card, she would have used that two-by-three inch little piece of orange-and-white plastic to buy a Holiday Inn!

She unzipped a small pocket in the lining of her

bag, hoping to find some hidden wealth. Her fingers hit a piece of metal. Slowly it slid into her palm—Robert MacDougal's apartment key. Abby stared at it for an interminable length of time.

Here was her lifeline, the key to a calm and peaceful haven. Richmond was a little over one hundred miles away. She had a full tank of gas. The money would provide her with food and a few necessary items of clothing until she was able to make a rational decision.

With calm precision Abby carefully reorganized her purse. She smoothed out her dress and started the engine. The Toyota gently eased itself into the flow of traffic with an outwardly self-composed driver behind the wheel.

CHAPTER TWELVE

Abby pushed the scrambled eggs into a ring design around the edge of her plate. Wryly, she wondered how high her cholesterol count was after eating nothing but eggs and cheese and crackers for five days. She grimaced, her lackluster gray eyes focusing on the opposite kitchen wall. There a collection of seven clocks formed a unique wall grouping. From the large functional modern design to a small wooden coach clock, they all agreed on the time—one o'clock in the morning. And she was eating. She laughed bitterly. What was she eating? Dinner? Breakfast? Time seemed inconsequential. Minutes and hours fused into days that had no names. Life had become as stale and tasteless as the food she was forcing herself to eat. She pushed the plate away, her hands cradling her bowed head.

The past week had been spent in self-examination

and Abby hated what she saw. She had been humiliated by a man—not once, but twice. Perhaps the first time could be excused to youth, but this time?

Not this time, she thought bitterly. This time she had eagerly swallowed whispered words of love, invited intimate caresses, and willingly shared her thoughts and dreams.

Would she ever forget Nick and the uncontrolled passion he had stirred within her? Would she be haunted for all time by the memory of his warm, rugged body, the brown eyes that could melt her bones? She could feel his skilled hands caressing her flesh, smell the sensuous maleness of his skin, taste his lips on hers.

"Damn it," she cried, "why can't I hate that man? Why can't I destroy my feelings for him the way he tried to destroy me?" She bit her bottom lip, willing her mind and body to neutralize him into objectivity. It was a futile effort that left her drained.

Wearily she picked up her plate, scraping the contents into the sink's garbage disposal, listening as the food was pulverized into oblivion. Abby walked slowly through the dark dining room, its glass-and-chrome table and mirrored hutch reflecting the moonlight that filtered through the sheer draperies. She paused on the threshold of the guest room, looking at the rumpled bed with loathing.

Each night had been the same. She would toss and twist in fitful, fragmented dreams. The nightmares crept in with disturbing regularity. Once again she was subjected to tormenting visions of the past that sent silent screams of terror echoing through her mind, reducing her tears to pitiful whimperings of pain. Worst were the dreams in which Dominick Maxwell Bennett presided, humiliating replays of a month of false happiness and shared caresses.

Again she felt the burning ache of emptiness sear through her veins. She had fallen in love with a facade, a carefully cultivated image that a man had projected. Everything had seemed so real, so honest. He had seemed so loving. Had it all been just to satisfy his male ego? Abby raked unsteady fingers through her limp, damp curls.

She remembered how intimately he had touched her, how she had begged him to make love to her. She began to tremble. She felt cheap and dirty. Abby quickly stripped off her blue cotton T-shirt and terry cloth shorts and ran into the bathroom. The fine shower spray sent warm cleansing needles of water over her perspiration-soaked body.

She scrubbed herself roughly with a soapy washcloth, ridding her skin of the memory of his hands and lips. But feelings didn't wash down the drain as easily as the soapsuds did, and soon the salty taste of tears mingled with the fresh water on her cheeks.

She leaned against the tile walls, all her strength drained away. It was as though her vital parts had been removed. She didn't know how long this self-flagellation could continue. She didn't remember feeling this demoralized when she had found out the truth about Eric. *That was because you didn't love Eric,* her mind echoed. My God, she thought wretchedly, even now when her passion had turned to pain, she was still in love with the man. It was degrading the way she still felt about Nick. Where was her pride?

Abby wrapped herself in a wide bath sheet and crossed over to the ornate mirror on the large Georgian dresser. A pale, hollow-eyed figure stared back at her. Could that really be her? Her lacerated emotions had done a brutal job on her physical health.

"From now on, I start thinking about myself," she vowed to her reflection. She refused to live one more day in a vacuum. She wasn't some inanimate object that needed taking care of. She was a survivor.

Something snapped in Abby. Her self-esteem rose as her defiance and anger grew stronger. For the first time in five days she thought about the bookshop.

Aunt Emily had run that shop for fifteen years and had enough confidence in Abby's ability to will it to her. She wasn't going to walk away. Not this time. She had done nothing wrong.

All she wanted was a release from Charge-X's credit system. She had copies of all the correspondence she'd sent. All right, she had repunched their lousy data cards, but that was only to get their attention.

Why, she had nurtured that bookshop with loving hands and she wasn't going to let a computer dehumanize her. She was no faceless piece of plastic.

A hidden spark of fire ignited in Abby's veins, blazing her spirit into action. Her eyes fell on a small paperweight sitting on the dresser. It was the state seal of Virginia—a woman warrior standing triumphant over tyranny.

She'd go down fighting, all the way to court if she

had to. No computer—no man—was going to intimidate her. By the time she got through with Dominick Maxwell Bennett and Charge-X they'd think the eruption of Mt. St. Helens was a burp!

With this new assessment of the situation came a certain detachment, a certain hardness that restored and revitalized her drained emotions. Abby picked up the small extension telephone and viciously punched out a number.

The clamor of her bedside telephone fully aroused Claire from a restless, uneasy sleep. "Hello," she whispered, switching on the reading lamp attached to her headboard.

"Mom."

"Oh, God. Abby! How are you? Where are you? I've been sick wondering where you've been. Are you all right?" Her words tumbled out in a sob of relief.

Abby gave a weak laugh. "I'm sorry. I didn't know how long I was going to be gone. I—I'm fine. Really."

Claire's knuckles whitened as her fingers tightened their hold on the yellow receiver. "Abby, I want you to come home." She paused and took a deep breath. "Nick's left. He's gone from the cottage. There's no reason for you not to come back here."

"He's . . . he's left?"

"Yes," her mother repeated firmly, sitting up in bed. "Do you need money or help getting home? I want you to come home, Abby." The silence on the other end of the line was deafening. "Abby!" Claire shouted in alarm.

"I'm still here, Mom. No . . . no, I don't need anything. I'll be home by late afternoon. Good night, Mom, and please don't worry." Abby stared at the phone with unseeing eyes. Nick had gone. She should be happy, but a cold numbness crept over her body. She crawled back into the rumpled, twisted bed, pulling the blankets and spread around her.

Claire clutched the buzzing receiver tightly in her hand until gentle fingers pried it free. John slid an arm around her shoulders, drawing her head against his bare chest. She relaxed against the comforting sound of his heart and the strength of his arms.

"Is Abby all right?" he asked quietly, stroking her rumpled hair with a caressing palm.

"She says she is. She sounded so alone, so scared." Claire raised her moist hazel eyes to his. "She sounded like I did a long time ago."

He rubbed her neck gently. "Will she come home?"

She nodded. "She wouldn't tell me where she was, but she said she could get here by late tomorrow afternoon."

"Why did you tell her—"

Claire sat up. "I just wanted my daughter home, John. If lying will accomplish that—"

The bedroom door flew open. "I thought I heard the phone. Was it . . . was it," Nick stammered, raking an agitated hand through his dark hair.

"Yes, it was Abby," his father told him with undisguised relief. "She's coming home tomorrow."

"How did she sound? Do you think she's all right?

Where is she?" Nick swallowed convulsively, shoving his hands into the patch pockets of his blue bathrobe, and pacing back and forth.

Claire shrugged her shoulders. "She wouldn't tell me where she was. She only said she was fine, but her voice . . . I don't know, she sounded scared. I never heard Abby sound so afraid." She looked at Nick and bit her lower lip. "I told her you had left Gull Cottage. I hope you can straighten out this entire mess." She leveled a stern but motherly gaze at him.

"Don't worry about it, I can handle Abby," he returned evenly, trying to convince not only her but himself as a succession of gnawing doubts kept encroaching on his mind. "Why didn't you tell Abby I was staying here?"

"We'll let you do all the telling, son," his father said firmly. "And, just for future reference, would you please knock before you enter our room? There's no telling what your new mother and I might be doing."

Nick laughed for the first time in a week. He kissed Claire on the cheek and wished both his parents a good night, then wandered back into Abby's bedroom. He removed his robe and slid his long, rugged body between the yellow gingham sheets on her narrow bed. The delicate scent of jasmine bath powder assailed his senses and he found it impossible to control the reaction his body had to the thought of seeing Abby tomorrow.

He settled back against the mattress, staring up at the eerie succession of shadows that danced on the moonlit ceiling. Each contorted demon of the night instantly reminded him of the pain and suffering Abby was experiencing.

I can handle Abby. His own words haunted him. He chewed his lower lip nervously, feeling his confidence flee. Could he handle Abby? Would he be able to convince her of his love? Would she trust him and feel secure enough to continue their relationship?

He rolled over and punched the pillows. "Damn," he swore out loud. "If only I had started with the truth." Somehow Nick knew he'd find no peaceful sleep tonight.

CHAPTER THIRTEEN

Abby sat on the wide, padded window seat in her bedroom staring, her gray eyes moist, a soft droop at the corners of her vulnerable mouth. She had been sitting there for quite some time, trying not to think, but the view from her window made that task impossible. Her gaze once again strayed back to the window—back to Gull Cottage. A dark, silent, empty Gull Cottage. She sniffed, wondering if it was possible to die from a broken heart.

A sharp rap on the door caused her to hastily rub her eyes. She quickly uncurled her long legs and moved toward her dresser.

"Abby." Her mother gave her a tremulous smile as she entered the room. "You're not planning to stay in here forever, are you?"

"No. No, of course not, Mom." She laughed lightly, pulling open a drawer and extracting her bathing suit. "I was going out for a sunset swim. I really missed the ocean while I was away."

"I wish Robert had been there for you. It does help to talk," Claire told her haltingly.

Abby gave her mother a wide, brilliant smile, not realizing that the haunted look in her eyes betrayed her true feelings. "I'm fine, really. I just needed to get away, that's all. I'm right back to normal." Her voice cracked and she hastily cleared her throat.

Claire ran her tongue over dry lips. "I—I saw how shocked you were over my marrying John." Her fingers nervously pleated the side of her beige print sundress.

"I was surprised, Mom, I have to admit that," Abby said evenly, tossing her bathing suit onto her bed. "I presume *he* told you exactly who he was and—"

"John is not your enemy, darling," Claire interrupted quickly, noting the angry tone in her daughter's voice.

"I'm afraid he might be yours."

"I don't understand . . ."

Abby sighed, walked over to Claire, and placed her hands on her mother's shoulders. "I love you, Mom, and I don't want you hurt again. I just see too many parallels between Dad and John Bennett. I don't think I can—"

"There is no comparison, Abby," Claire told her forcefully. "Your father and I had problems right from the beginning of our marriage. I was very young and in love with love. I thought his strong, silent image was very romantic. My world revolved around my house and later my daughters. I honestly never noticed how far your father had drifted away. That's why everything hit me so hard." She stopped and was silent for a moment. Then Claire smiled, her eyes radiating a joy Abby had never seen before. "John and I have a wonderful relationship. I admit I was quite surprised when he told me who he was. But I was adult enough not to run away. We were able to talk about it and, as a result, it brought us even closer together." She leveled an accusing gaze at her daughter.

Abby pulled away, swallowing the lump in her throat that threatened to strangle her. "My . . . my problem with Nick is totally different," she quickly defended herself. "I didn't run away. I just needed to get away and think things out."

Claire sighed and ran her fingers carelessly through her hair. "I suppose I should have waited to get married. It would have been better to have a family discussion, put all the facts on the table. Eloping seems rather childish." Her voice trailed off miserably.

"Oh, Mom, I'm sorry. I never meant to dampen your happiness." Abby slid her arms around her mother's waist and gave her a hug. "It's very obvious that John loves you and, just looking at you, I know how much you love him. At least he was honest with you. That's the most important part of a relationship —honesty." She turned her head toward the window, trying to stop the tears that burned against her eyelids. "Dee is going to think eloping to Maryland is very romantic, although she'll wail for weeks about missing it." She managed another bright smile.

"Well," Claire conceded ruefully, "when we called and told her we got married, among all the joyous squeals there were a few moans. We did manage to convince her to finish out her two weeks in Washington."

"I guess having me around the house takes the edge off your at-home honeymoon." Abby grimaced self-consciously.

"John's planning to take me on a trip in a few weeks, although he's being very secretive about where we're going." She laughed lightly. "Dee will be back by then and can give you a hand at the bookshop." She paused, waiting for Abby's reaction. She sighed when none was forthcoming. "Abby, what about you?"

"Me?" She shrugged her shoulders indifferently and wandered back to her dresser. She picked up a hairbrush and pulled it roughly through her matted curls. "I guess I'll take one day at a time. I came home ready to fight for the store, but it seems I've no one to fight with." She swallowed again, then concentrated on her reflection in the mirror, pretending not to see the dark shadows that marred her features. "Don't worry about me, I'll pull through. I did before." Her nerveless fingers let the brush clatter noisily onto the dresser top. "I've been thinking about moving to an apartment in town."

"An apartment? But why, Abby?"

"You and John deserve privacy. Having Dee here will be more than enough," Abby continued hastily.

174

"I was thinking you could knock down the wall between Dee's and my room and make one large bedroom-sitting room and Dee could have your old room. You—you are planning on staying here, aren't you?"

Claire nodded. "John loves it here. You are right, we could do with some remodeling, and that's a very interesting idea." She paused. "It's hard for you to be here with John, isn't it?"

"Don't worry about it," Abby smiled. "Listen, I better take my swim before it gets too dark to find the water."

Claire gave her daughter a comforting hug. It took Abby just a few minutes to wriggle into her maillot. She padded out into the living room, still tying the halter neck strings. "Mom, I can't seem to find my beach jacket," she called. Her voice abruptly died in her throat at the sight of Dominick Maxwell Bennett sitting on the living room sofa.

Abby's eyes darted wildly from him to her mother to his father, her breath coming in quick, nervous gulps. She struggled to get her words out. "I thought you said he'd left."

"I left Gull Cottage," Nick corrected, his voice a low, seductive drawl. "I've been sleeping here. As a matter of fact, I've been using your room . . . your bed."

The living room seemed to shrink as he rose from the couch. He looked tall and sleek and as dangerous as a panther in dark, tight-fitting trousers and a knit shirt. She failed to notice the suggestion of pallor beneath the bronze of his face and the dark hollows under his eyes that matched her own.

"My bed." Abby fairly choked on the words. Her back stiffened, her eyes flashing with fury. "Did you charge my room on your credit card, Mr. Bennett? Is this what they call the final kill?" she exploded sarcastically, completely oblivious to the other people in the room.

"Not in the least," Nick returned smoothly, his brown eyes possessively assessing her shapely figure in the copper swimsuit. "We've got a few things to iron out—"

She sucked in her breath sharply. "You're crazy," she snapped. "If you think—" She stopped, feeling an inherent danger from the dancing light in his eyes and the lazy smile curving on his lips. The muscles in her body constricted. Her whole being vibrated with a mixture of apprehension and elation. Abby's body screamed for action. She whirled and sprinted for the back door and the comparative safety of the beach.

Nick paused long enough to give his worried parents a rueful grin. "Don't bother waiting up," he called, his long legs eating up the distance between him and Abby.

It was extremely difficult to gain any speed in the soft, deep sand, so Abby changed direction until her feet encountered the hard-packed tidewater. She didn't have any idea where she was going, nor did she care. She only knew she was frightened of Nick and herself.

Abby's legs were literally pulled out from under

her by Nick's flying tackle, and both of them lay sprawling facedown in the water. She rolled over, angling for leverage, but found herself pinned beneath Nick's hard, muscular length. When his mouth moved against her jaw, she slammed her fists hard against his shoulders. Abby twisted her head, her body struggling wildly beneath him.

"I thought we could talk civilly." Nick breathed heavily, his face harshly cast in the dim evening light.

"Nothing you have to say could ever interest me," Abby choked angrily, cruelly trying to wedge her knee between his legs. "Nothing is going to make me forget what you did or forgive you."

"I guess I'll have to resort to my baser instincts," he said in a dangerously low voice. She lay perfectly still, compressing her lips into a tight, mutinous line. Nick stood up, pulling her with him, and swung her over his shoulder, fireman-style.

Abby's fists pummeled against his broad back. "Put me down! This isn't going to work. I'm not going to listen to you!"

"Settle down, Abby," he cautioned. "I've got a few things to say to you and you're damn well going to listen!" Nick pulled open the screen door of Gull Cottage and walked through the darkened kitchen into the living room, dumping her unceremoniously onto the plush cream-colored sofa. He reached over and switched on the reading lamp, keeping his other hand flat against the base of her throat.

They were both breathing hard. Abby's gray eyes were round and wary, her face set and forbidding. Neither of them spoke.

Abby saw a devilish glint appear in Nick's brown eyes, a crooked smile on his well-shaped mouth. Hypnotized, she watched his lips move closer to hers. Angry, she twisted her head to one side. "What kind of tormenting game are you playing now?" she hurled bitterly.

There was grimness in his determination. He lifted his hand from her body and settled himself on the edge of the sofa. "I'm not playing any game. I never was—"

"Don't lie to me," Abby snapped, pushing herself off the couch. "You came here for only one reason. You and your lousy company can go to hell."

Nick reached up, grabbed her arm, and pulled her back onto the cushions. "You're judging me on another woman's accusations," he advised her sharply.

"They were facts," she hurled at him explosively, twisting her wrist from his grasp. She curled herself into a self-contained ball against the sofa arm.

"They were half-truths at best," he countered. His voice was quiet and controlled. "I'm not the president of Charge-X anymore. I sold the company."

"What?" her voice cracked. She turned her luminous eyes toward him. Her heart beat an uneven rhythm in her breast as she stared at him.

Nick ran a hand around his neck, uncomfortably pulling at his wet, muddy shirt. "When I took the manuscript to New York, I also made arrangements to merge Charge-X with a bigger credit agency. Both Dad and I have severed all ties with both companies. I'm surprised you didn't get a letter from them— with an apology," he told her gently.

Abby licked her dry lips, remembering the official-looking envelope that had come in the mail last Saturday, a letter she had failed to open. "That doesn't alter the fact that you initially came down here to—"

"I came down here," he interrupted, "for two reasons. I needed a rest. When my father retired, he put me in charge of a company I never wanted to run. I'm a writer, not a businessman. After running Charge-X for over a year, I became disgusted with myself. It was very easy to become drunk with power and its privileges."

"What was the other reason?" Abby whispered, her eyes focusing with intense concentration on an imaginary spot on the pale blue wall.

Nick's long fingers gently cupped her chin, turning her tear-stained face toward his own. "Charge-X owed one Miss Abigail Wetherby an apology for ignoring her letters. Although what you did to those computers . . ." His voice trailed off when she failed to respond to his humorous rejoinder. "I admit I should have told you right from the start who I was. Delaying the truth somehow makes it more difficult to tell."

"That . . . that woman, Marie," Abby stammered. "She said—"

"She said a lot of things. A lot of lies," Nick continued, his voice taking on a hardness that made Abby shiver. "There was no way I could ever take your bookshop. You understand that, don't you?"

Abby nodded, her lips pressed tightly together.

"I spouted out a lot of placebos to soothe an overzealous computer-billing director, much the same way you agreed with that woman in your store about what books to display." Nick drew a deep breath. "Marie came to the shop to settle an old score. She wanted to hurt me and she knew the only way to do that was to hurt you. Apparently Dee had told her all about us and she just seized on that for her revenge."

"She's very beautiful," Abby said hesitantly, almost afraid to voice her thoughts about the dark-eyed blonde.

"I never said she wasn't. But that's all she has to offer," he stated in a cold voice. "How foolish I was to ever get involved with a woman like Marie." He winced, a sour taste forming in his mouth.

"She . . . she said you were . . . lovers."

"Not love, there was never any love. We had sex," he told her tersely. "They are two different emotions. Marie and I used each other. I'm not particularly proud of that part of my life. That's one of the reasons I wanted to get away." His voice wavered. He looked at her with a bleakness in his eyes that she'd never seen before. "I would give anything if all that never happened. Can you ever forgive me?"

Abby turned her head, her voice a low sob. "I spent a week on the verge of mental suicide. That . . . that horrible scene in the shop sent me back four years in time. I thought I had conquered all those nightmares, all those ghosts, but I hadn't. They just came rushing back, along with new ones. It was the ultimate rejection. I was so hurt, so confused. I

. . . I—" She couldn't go on. Tears were running in thick rivulets down her cheeks.

Nick reached over and picked up her cold, trembling hand. "My God, I don't think I'll ever be able to forgive myself for putting you through that. If you had just come back. I wanted to explain things to you. I should have told the truth right from the start, I know that. I don't know how things got so confused. I've been so worried about you, I thought I'd go out of my mind." His chest expelled a heavy sigh. "I love you, Abby. I think I fell in love with you the very first time I saw you. There you were standing in your shop, a smudge of dirt on your cheek, the light of battle in your eyes, and I suddenly found myself wanting a total stranger."

She refused to look at him, laying her wet cheek against the sofa cushion and closing her eyes. "I'm afraid of you." Her voice shook. "I'm frightened at how easily the right words flow from your lips, how honest your eyes look. You lie so well."

Nick dropped her hand, then stood up and thrust both his hands into his trouser pockets. He walked over to the window, staring into the dark night, a feeling of emptiness in his heart. "I've lost you, haven't I? You've got to believe that I love you, Abby. Ask yourself why I waited for you, why I didn't go back to New York, why I care so much. I love you. Can that mean anything?"

Abby stared at Nick's bowed head, his shoulders slumped dejectedly. He was as vulnerable as she was. He had told her once to take out the past, look at it, and put it back forever. But could she really trust him, believe his declaration of love? Would she forever have doubts about his fidelity? If she really loved him, wouldn't she settle for less than perfection and make allowances for his weaknesses? They had such an intense attraction for each other. A sharing, a caring. To believe in his love would reenforce her trust in their relationship and cement their future. The ghosts of her past still haunted her, taunting her with humiliation.

Nick heard her footsteps. He closed his eyes, feeling an icy desolation course through his veins, and waited for the sound of a closing door. Abby was leaving. And with her she'd take his heart and soul.

Soft arms wrapped around his waist. His eyes flew open as Abby pressed herself tightly against him, hugging him as if she were afraid he'd disappear. "Dominick Maxwell Bennett." Her voice was a low throb in his ear. "I love you very much. I want to be a part of your life."

He turned, his arms capturing her in a savage embrace. His mouth hungrily devoured her softly parted lips. Abby melted with undisguised abandon against the hard body of the man she loved. His lips caressed every inch of her face, his fingers lovingly tangled in her curls. Her senses soared under the slow, sweet arousal only this man could bring. Happiness threatened to explode within her.

Her fingers reached out to trace the sensuous line of his firmly molded mouth. The days of not being with him, of not touching him suddenly made her own desire uncontrollable. Her hands curled around his neck, dragging his head down to her waiting lips.

She was breathless and trembling when he finally lifted his head.

"You've been gone too long," Nick told her, his voice a husky tremor. "From now on, whenever we have a fight, you get no farther than the beach. I was so scared. I never expected you to disappear. I had no one to call. I was worried that you might have had an accident and been in the hospital."

Abby's arms were clasped tightly around his waist. She burrowed against him. "I didn't have anyplace to go and no money. For one instant, I even wished for a Charge-X card to charge a hotel room and food." She grinned wryly.

"I'm glad you had Robert's apartment, although in the future," he cautioned gruffly, "in the future, just remember that I love you very much." His lips once again captured hers, as if to drive away all the painful memories.

A shower of dry sand cascaded onto the carpet. Nick's hand lifted her face up to his; a devilish glint lit up his eyes. "Come on, I'll help you shower off all that sand and salt."

"Who could possibly be calling this early?" Abby grumbled sleepily, turning in the wide brass bed to snuggle against Nick's warm body. She slid her smooth, silky leg intimately between his long muscular ones while her hand slid lovingly down his naked chest to settle on his hip. She listened with half-wakened attention to his conversation, smothering a yawn after he hung up the receiver.

"That was my father congratulating me for clearing up our disagreement," he told her huskily, his hands sliding possessively over her soft curves, his lips moving slowly over her jaw line, down the curve of her throat to seek the scented hollow between her breasts.

Abby gave a contented sigh, her hands brushing lightly over his broad back to tangle in the dark, thick hair at the nape of his neck. "He could have called a little later. We didn't get much sleep last night." She blushed, remembering the depth of their passion as Nick had taught her the new and exotic language of love between two bodies.

"Well," he murmured, smiling into her sleepy gray eyes, "while he is my father, he is also your new stepfather. And your new stepfather is threatening me with all sorts of bodily injury if I don't make an honest woman out of you. And he wants it done today." He kissed the tip of her nose, rolled off her and slid his hands under his head. "You know, I'd like to take you to Greece for a honeymoon. The folks can have their honeymoon while we wait for your passport. You can get your work caught up at the bookshop while I do some rewriting on my book. And when they get back, off we'll go. I also have another little surprise for you." His eyes danced in amusement.

"What's that?" she asked suspiciously.

He reached out and pulled her onto his chest, his hands fitting her pliant body into the hard contours of his own. "I bought Gull Cottage for us. I know you like the place and it seems perfect." He stopped, tipping his head to one side on the pillow and studying her closely. "You do like the house, don't you, Abby?"

She shook her head. "I love the house and I love you." She wriggled up on his chest, propping her elbows on either side of his head, worriedly gnawing her soft lower lip. "Nick, you're not marrying me because there's a shotgun at your back, are you? I mean you don't have to. I mean . . . I understand if you just want to live together. Some men just can't be married and I don't want you to feel trapped."

"That's very magnamimous of you, darling." He grinned, tumbling her back down on the mattress, his eyes holding her captive with a smoldering gaze. "I'm marrying you because I love you and I want you with me for a lifetime and"—he paused teasingly, his lips touching hers, their breath mingling as one—"so I don't have to change the dedication page on my novel."

"What?" Her eyes widened perceptively.

Nick reached over to pull open the bottom drawer of the night table and took out a piece of onion-skin paper from a folder. He looked down at the typewritten words and smiled.

Eight words were centered on the yellow page. "To Abby—my love, my life, my wife." Abby swallowed hard, her eyes shimmering with emotion. "You did this before you went to New York?"

At his affirmative nod, she slid her arms around his neck, her lips meeting his in a singular sweetness and expression of love that made him catch his breath.

* * *

185

The justice of the peace was delighted to marry the son and daughter of the same couple he had married just a week before. He didn't even mind the fact that they were over an hour late for the ceremony.

LOOK FOR NEXT MONTH'S CANDLELIGHT ECSTASIES:

Love—the way you want it!

Candlelight Romances

THE WILD ONE

by
MARIANNE HARVEY

bestselling author of *The Dark Horseman*
and *The Proud Hunter*

Proud, beautiful Judith—raised by her stern
grandmother on the savage Cornish coast—
boldly abandoned herself to one man and sought
solace in the arms of another. But only one man
could tame her, could match her fiery spirit,
could fulfill the passionate promise of rapturous,
timeless love.

A Dell Book $2.95   (19207-2)

THE DARK HORSEMAN

Marianne Harvey

author of *The Proud Hunter*

Beautiful Donna Penroze had sworn to her dying father that she would save her sole legacy, the crumbling tin mines and the ancient, desolate estate *Trencobban*. But the mines were failing, and Donna had no one to turn to. No one except the mysterious Nicholas Trevarvas—rich, arrogant, commanding. Donna would do anything but surrender her pride, anything but admit her irresistible longing for *The Dark Horseman*.

A Dell Book $3.25

The passionate sequel to
the scorching novel of
fierce pride and forbidden love

THE PROUD HUNTER

by Marianne Harvey

Author of *The Dark Horseman*
and *The Wild One*

Trefyn Connor—he demanded all that was his—and
more—with the arrogance of a man who fought to
win . . . with the passion of a man who meant to pos-
sess his enemy's daughter and make her pay the
price!

Juliet Trevarvas—the beautiful daughter of The Dark
Horseman. She would make Trefyn come to her. She
would taunt him, shock him, claim him body and soul
before she would surrender to THE PROUD HUNTER.

A Dell Book $3.25   (17098-2)

Dell Bestsellers

- [ ] **RANDOM WINDS** by Belva Plain $3.50 (17158-X)
- [ ] **MEN IN LOVE** by Nancy Friday $3.50 (15404-9)
- [ ] **JAILBIRD** by Kurt Vonnegut $3.25 (15447-2)
- [ ] **LOVE: Poems** by Danielle Steel $2.50 (15377-8)
- [ ] **SHOGUN** by James Clavell $3.50 (17800-2)
- [ ] **WILL** by G. Gordon Liddy $3.50 (09666-9)
- [ ] **THE ESTABLISHMENT** by Howard Fast.......$3.25 (12296-1)
- [ ] **LIGHT OF LOVE** by Barbara Cartland $2.50 (15402-2)
- [ ] **SERPENTINE** by Thomas Thompson $3.50 (17611-5)
- [ ] **MY MOTHER/MY SELF** by Nancy Friday $3.25 (15663-7)
- [ ] **EVERGREEN** by Belva Plain $3.50 (13278-9)
- [ ] **THE WINDSOR STORY**
  by J. Bryan III & Charles J.V. Murphy $3.75 (19346-X)
- [ ] **THE PROUD HUNTER** by Marianne Harvey ..$3.25 (17098-2)
- [ ] **HIT ME WITH A RAINBOW**
  by James Kirkwood $3.25 (13622-9)
- [ ] **MIDNIGHT MOVIES** by David Kaufelt $2.75 (15728-5)
- [ ] **THE DEBRIEFING** by Robert Litell $2.75 (01873-5)
- [ ] **SHAMAN'S DAUGHTER** by Nan Salerno
  & Rosamond Vanderburgh $3.25 (17863-0)
- [ ] **WOMAN OF TEXAS** by R.T. Stevens $2.95 (19555-1)
- [ ] **DEVIL'S LOVE** by Lane Harris $2.95 (11915-4)

At your local bookstore or use this handy coupon for ordering:

Dell **DELL BOOKS**
P.O. BOX 1000, PINEBROOK, N.J. 07058

Please send me the books I have checked above. I am enclosing $ _____
(please add 75¢ per copy to cover postage and handling). Send check or money order—no cash or C.O.D.'s. Please allow up to 8 weeks for shipment.

Mr/Mrs/Miss _____

Address _____

City _____ State/Zip _____